WHAT IF YOUR CRUSH SECRETLY LOVES YOU?

RESHMA GANTA

wovenwordspublishers
.com

Woven Words Publishers OPC Pvt. Ltd.

Registered Office:

Vill: Raipur, P.O: Raipur Paschimbar,

Dist: Purba Midnapore, Pin: 721401,

West Bengal, India.

Branch Office(Operations): Hyderabad

www.wovenwordspublishers.com

Email: publish@wovenwordspublishers.com

First published by Woven Words Publishers OPC Pvt. Ltd., 2020.

Price: 300/-

IMPRINT: WOVEN WORDS LAUNCHPAD

ISBN 13: 978-93-88762-24-3
ISBN 10: 93-88762-24-X

To my family,
for their incredible love and extensive support.

ACKNOWLEDGEMENTS

I would like to express my special thanks of gratitude to my parents, Adinarayana Ganta and Devi Ganta for giving me the strength to reach for the stars and chase my dreams. This is to let you know that I appreciate and love you my dearest brother, Revanth. You always try heart and soul in performing such duty towards me that money can't buy.

I am particularly grateful for the assistance given by my teachers and my friends, for their unwavering support. My well-wisher, Sai Pradeep Boddu deserve wholehearted thanks as well for being there in my journey of writing this book.

I thank my friend, Percy Preethi Dande for giving me the prettiest cover design. I would extend my thanks to my publisher Mosiur Rehman for his consistent faith in me and my writings.

If it is mobile that enslaved people then it is social media that brought out relations. Here is a story of a girl who is responsible, matured, and family-oriented encounters a phase of life called love. And love marked for its perenniality and purity had too many versions. The best version of it is obtained only when both accept themselves as they are! In this book, we will see the journey of two cute souls connected online. Will that destination be lovely or awful in the end?

CONTENTS

DREAMS DECIDE DESTINY?

It was roughly 10 am dawn. The sun, with all his superiority, made people clasp to their dwellings. I was crouching on a chair and speaking to a stranger who had well-combed, brownish-black silky hair, vast and raw eyebrows, beady, glint brown, rounded eyes. He had a refinement in the eyes with his incredible fair hue. He was in a black plain shirt with cuffed sleeves till elbow and his central neckband held high. Gloomy denim was making a decent combo. He wore well-polished sliders and he was certainly unusual. But his appearance was second to none. I was about to ask him something more crucial, then all of an abrupt, Parnika woke me up.

Aye, A dream! And Parnika, my roommate.

She cared a hoot about me in the entire college. She became a walking encyclopedia realizing everything pertaining me backward and forwards. I being matter-of-fact, barely believed in species and she was one among those few. I aroused from my mattress and

she shrieked at me, "It is 7:30 a.m and you didn't even scrub your teeth."

I got up striding near to the wall in search of my toothbrush then

Parnika asked, "What are you searching for?"

I mumbled, "Brush," with my drowsy voice.

She whirled me back to my ledge and handed my tongue purifier, scrub with paste. I was still in the utopia of that hallucination and didn't make a move.

"It is 8' O clock we are supposed to attend the class. Why are you parked and what will this position fetch you?" she yelled.

Heeding that, I whisked into the washroom with a towel and my costume. I attired in my uniform, a blue-blazed white top with a blue-colored dupatta strictly folded and the equivalent colored bottom. I loaded my backpack and held it to one of my shoulders, picked the *Amygdalus Communis,* confused? So-called Almonds that I moistened in water the previous dusk, and with another hand was my room lock. I called out Parnika and we steered to the mess.

On my path, I was peeling off the almonds and narrating her, my dream that I had last night. She argued, how am I that innocent to take all my dreams so serious. I initiated one of the happenings that took place in my family to justify my talk. My mum once said that she dreamt of uniting an unknown. My brother and I inquired if she could remember any of his traits, surprisingly, she pointed towards my papa! So I am the kind of girl who believes in fantasies as a prognosis for something to happen ahead.

Just as our talk broadened, we reached the mess, had breakfast, *oil-soaked poories, uncooked potato kurma*, and *watered coffee*. I always stuffed that worthless food just to complement my stomach and we started back to our classrooms. They aren't too far, it just takes seconds to reach. I held my bag balancing on both the shoulders and handed Parnika's drafter. As she was a Mechanical student, she would have the use of drafter and rather a Computer science student like I wouldn't!

I reached my class. It was Sathwika, who greeted me loud as I entered. She would always spare a place for me to sit and much close to me than anyone else in the classroom. She is quite a funny, cheerful girl whom I have ever come across, moreover, she is the most liked girl in the class. She had impressive eyes and amiable demeanor. I enjoyed her company throughout the class.

We were listening to the sermon that Monday forenoon. It was a crazy habit that I and Sathwika had, to fall hunger in the very second hour. We laughed in the middle of the class whenever I do a comical gesture with my hand on my tummy, moving it in a circular direction. I was frequently checking my mobile for the hours hand to strike 1:00 p.m. And time, when I wanted it to stride fast, it would pause, and when I wanted it to cut short, it would seriously move fast. This punctuality is the best thing that I adore about it. It would neither halt nor hop for somebody. However every day, in this circumstance, I would loathe it! My belly was touching my back!

We were then left out with half an hour. Then, my phone flickered, and it was some Instagram follower request, I tapped in. The account read *ram_virat* on the screen and the name was Ram. It was a public account and I checked in for his followers and following. Surprisingly, he followed no girl and no girl followed him. What kind of a specie he was? I marveled. Then, I rendered my memory to a day when Karthik once said that, he had a mate named Ram who hails from the same townlet that he does.

By the way, Karthik is a very good pal of mine and a bit close to my pal circle. I had to mention this here, Karthik is my PUC (Pre-University Course just like regular intermediate) classmate. He was one of the supportive friends I had. In the very initial meeting of ours, we were defending as if Tom and Jerry. With time, we were pointed out to be the best friends. Literally, his friendship strengthened me.

In general, I have a strategy of not ratifying the uncommon requests. Seeing Karthik following him, I accepted Ram's plea. Besides, he was Karthik's friend. I kept my phone aside and was back to my agony. There was pop out on my mobile screen, it was imploring me for a confirmation whether to let

Ram text me, a security query by Instagram like it does to all the other users. I accepted. The very next moment, my mobile flashed the arrival of a message.

He texted, "Hai."

I corroborated, "You are Karthik's friend right?"

He then said, "Yeah, I am."

He inquired, "Isn't your class on?"

I said, "Yeah it is going but I am not interested to listen."

I fibbed but didn't tell him that I am freaking hungry.

My time had come, it was 1:00 p.m. I left my phone on the desk and was rushing near the door with Sathwika, then a group of girls from the ECE Department were heading towards us saying that, the mess is quite rush. I turned into the water, heavily roasted!

The famished me held phone, lying on the table. Then, received the text from him.

"Why didn't you have lunch yet?" he asked.

I retorted, "The girls' mess was flooded with people so I couldn't !"

I then questioned him, "Are you within my vision!?"

He said, "I peeped into your class while I was going to mess."

I then asked him to have lunch and was out of chat.

It was rats in my breadbasket! A ravenous appetite it was, so creepy!

It was after 15 minutes, we were a group of six people who would generally go to the mess and one among the group raised her voice that she was hungry, I joined her mine, then Sathwika, one after the other, we started singing a song that generated a chain reaction among the rest! Whatever it may be, we thought of heading to mess. As it was Monday, our menu was egg fried rice, the only food that I consume two serving spoons.

My pals would make fun of me having so little food like a baby, Sathwika would always say that her neighbor, a three-year-old kid would consume more than me and so I am. I take everything lite. We were done with our lunch, and my rats were dozing peacefully. And I, along with Sathwika and gang began back to our classroom. It was my class girls who had a playlist on their laptops and were playing it loud in the class. I came back to my position tapping my legs to the beat and took my mobile out. I was about to play criminal case but I scrolled down my widget checking if I had any notifications to clear. I found his notification,

He asked, "Had lunch?"

I said, "Yeah, I had."

He then inquired, "Veg or non-veg?"

I retorted, "Non-veg obviously."

He asked, "Are you a non-veg lover?"

I said, "I crave."

I asked, "Do you know me?"

He said, "I know you from our PUC."

Along with that,

He added, "You are MIDHUNA, your identity number is S360223, then your living place is Kakinada."

Then he even added my dad's name, later my prior Instagram ID, followed by a happening that I didn't expect that from him. The incident was, he first saw me in an examination hall where I, along with my friend speaking to a professor after the exam and I wore white and white clothing with a black-designed print at the pretty bottom of my top. He was very particular about my outfit too.

I was struck dumb, I didn't know what to tell him later. With all my novelty,

"Why did you know everything about me?" I inquired him.

"I am just interested," he simply curtailed the response.

It caused a fuss in my heart and asked, "Would you mind sending me your picture?"

He asked me for a minute. I waited, then loaded the picture, he sent me an image with his companions and

He mentioned, "I am the third one from the left."

"I am not so clear with your face in this pic. Will, you send me another one?" I sent another text.

With no answer, he sent me another photograph, that is much clear.

I was out of blue watching the picture, it was him, damn him, who was with me in my dream last night!!!!!!!

CRUSH!?

As the class started, I locked my phone and zipped my bag with my mobile in. My thoughts flew to a day when I was looking into profiles of my contacts on WhatsApp, I halted at Karthik's profile. It was Karthik along with a cute gentleman in a white shirt. He had some allure in his eyes. There again, we had a chat about him. And he was Ram, that dude in my dream. Karthik said that Ram got a female friend request on Facebook and she had an enormous crush on him. There arose a day-to-day talk between them and she was named Praveenya. So, then, I began searching for Praveenya that day, I inquired several people but of no benefit.

One fine day, I was waiting near the water point to restore my bottle and someone called out loud,

"Praveenya, are you done?" She, who was in front of me is that girl.

She was just run-of-the-mill, barely to my height, not so prolonged hair, and was fairly menial to him that he would merit someone much better.

Then my thoughts were disturbed by Sathwika, calling me out for a break. We both had a couple of unique spots to prowl in the intermission. I was the class of girls who would not hoist head as I saunter in the populace, is that shy? No! Not at all but, I feel highly comfortable and aware of the fact that a person's gait can say a lot about their character, so I watch how I carry myself. We went to the place which was a few strides away from our classroom. No one would notice us there, so we spent time resting and performing all the idiotic stuff.

That day, I plucked some blossoms and randomly hurled them on the ground. Then, we got to be CBI! Our childish acts would not get such a prominent name. I would start the investigation like this, so the flowers were lying in 45 degrees curve, which indicates the felon has assigned this direction for his seizure. Then he sauntered two steps ahead, there again, we could uncover some handprints on the wall, which implies he had some enormous chore done so he would kneel to the wall.

Listening to all my senseless talk, Sathwika reminded me time, and we hurried to the classroom. We were a fraction delayed but my educator permitted us into class with no offense. We sat in our places and then I took out my mobile, I had a few notifications, one from criminal case asking me to tap there to imprison the fugitive, then, club factory persuading me to go on 50% off for a festive sale, next, were few WhatsApp messages from random groups, later was his text on Instagram. Typically, when we wish to know about someone, we do ask what else.

He asked, "What else?"

I had nothing to say, without disappointing him, I questioned, "Karthik and you studied the same school?"

He replied, "Yea, in fact, it is almost ten years relation we had."

So there went on some sedentary conversation, nothing much interesting. And it was 5:00 in the sundown and we were done with our classes and have to vacate. With no hesitation, I packed my bag. I would not stay back in the classroom once the chronograph strikes 5:00 p.m. I pulled out Sathwika and we were walking to our dormitories.

I am a kind of loquacious girl and would not spare a second to anyone. I was banging pranks in between. Nevertheless, my pranks weren't that satisfactory as Sathwika's. She lifts me when I am unhappy and she keeps me out of all my fears and she always cracks me up. With all my logicless jokes, we reached our dorms. As I reached my room, I placed my bag on my bed and was searching for Parnika. I asked Nila, my other roommate. I have a good relationship with her but I am not too intimate.

Nila pointed towards the restrooms. As she did, I could remember the clothes that I had to wash. The vastest concern for me all through my hostel life was rinsing my clothes. Sometimes, I moan calling my mum about this. Anyways, I went to the battlefield.

I even had a shower and came to my room. I unzipped my bag, took my mobile out, turned the volume up from silent mode, and charged it. I got ready to mess on casual wear. Parnika and Nila didn't turn up. So, I started doing my class assignments. There hit a notification on my mobile screen, it was from Ram on Instagram,

He initiated, "What's up?"

I told, "I am working with my assignment."

He then asked, "What else?"

I said, "It's your turn."

He added many flirting statements to the conversation.

I inquired, "Are you on a rehearsal for a movie?"

"I didn't get you!" he said.

"Your dialogues are so cinematic," I added.

"I am true, by the way, I don't watch movies. Do you?" he asked.

"No, even I'm not interested in movies," I stated.

So then I ended the chat as we were leaving to mess. I had dinner along with Parnika and Nila. Striding back to the dorm, we were sharing all those crazy things that happened in our respective classrooms. And then, I said Parnika about my dream boy. I mean, the boy in the dream had texted me. She was striking off my words, moreover, not at all ready to believe. Then, I made a clear picture for her.

Making myself comprehensible made me sip a bottle of water in a single attempt. So, we were back to our room, I took my mobile, called my mom as usual and spoke to her for an hour. She is the only one who would listen to all my silly stuff with a lot of patience. Then I called my dad, it won't take much time like my mom's call, it's just very few minutes conversation. I finished the call. I logged into Instagram, it was his notification on the top.

He initiated the conversation, "Had dinner?"

I replied, "Yeah, and you?"

In between, Karthik called me and was speaking to me all about his class that day. And I said to him about the new contact that I had. He started cultivating some fun between Ram and me. He gave me a hint of using the name HARINI near him. And he wanted me to get to know his response. I was perplexed but I said okay having lost my bearings. As the conversation began,

I asked, "Who is Harini?"

"How do you know her? Is it that idiot who said you to question me?" he texted.

"Idiot? I wonder who that idiot you referring to?" I replied.

"Your friend, Karthik," he stated.

"How come you knew that it is Karthik who pushed me to ask you this?" I interrogated.

"Just a wild guess," he said.

"Guess! I don't think so. Are you guys pre-planned?" I inquired.

"Aaare nothing like that Midhuna," he responded.

"Then, what is the reason behind your perfect guessing?" I questioned.

"It is only Karthik who knew about Harini. So I asked you," he admitted.

"Fine, now tell me. Who is this Harini?" I asked.

He suspended the conversation for two minutes and then came out with the reply.

He responded, "Harini, my tenth classmate, I used to speak to her a lot and even she does."

I said, "If this is the only thing, I wouldn't have asked you. Open up, man."

He responded, "Furthermore, I used to have a crush on her."

"It was just till my schooling," he added.

He didn't let me give a text and again messaged me that, "She had a boyfriend right now and I have no feelings for her," he alarmed.

I started shouting in unison Harini's name, making fun and didn't let him wrap up his affidavit. So then, he said that he would tell me something more fascinating and found a way to stop me. I was pounding him for what he was about to tell me. I seemed like a pampered kid near him. At that moment when I was making hell over there, he didn't even terminate my words in between. He behaved with too much tolerance.

He then said, "I have a crush in the college."

"Is it? Who is she?" I asked.

"Give a guess," he challenged. "She is short but cute," I interrupted, "Is she Yamini?"

"No, she is fair, had a stunning smile and all that steers me are those dimples when she smiles," he said.

"She is Ashritha for sure. Am I correct?"

His text dropped a bombshell.

"You do possess all those characteristics, and your dimples do magic. It's you whom I am crushing on," he threw me into a waterless well.

It was a bolt from the blue. I asked him twice for confirmation. He confirmed it's ME!

INTO THE NEXT LEVEL

"A crush and the toothbrush must be altered every three months, one of the unknown authors said," I texted him this way.

"You and that unknown author have no brain at all to speak all this stuff," he answered back. "By the way, it's been three years I am staring you and if it was a crush, it would have changed within this era," he added.

"Three years!" I exclaimed.

"I said you right, that I know you from PUC and even had a crush on you. You know what I am good at?" he questioned.

"What?" I asked.

"Getting caught to your friend when I am staring you," he said hilariously.

"To my friend!? and who is that?" inquired him with a lot of novelty.

He said, "She is tall and she would company you everywhere. I couldn't specifically memorize her name but I'll surely tell you. And, I was seriously caught to her every time possible."

After 5 minutes, "RENUKA is her name," he said as if he won a citation.

Till that day, I was skeptical about him and guessed he was flirting. That evening, Renuka, came to my room like she did every day. Renuka was another promising friend of mine. She believes me extensively and would always have the final talk with me before she goes to bed. And I meant plenty to her.

I asked her displaying his portrait from my phone, "Renu, do you know him?"

As shortly as she saw his picture, "This man! he just glues his eyes at people fleeing the world behind and found him staring at our side too various times. How come his picture is with you?" she interrogated.

I narrated the entire story to her and she then realized, all that he glares was at ME and was hooked more than a hundred times to her. And then, she chuckled recalling the way he used to peep from the bushes and relating that it was all to me. That day, she wasn't sure to whom he was gawking. Today, she is much obvious. This made me built an embankment of trust towards him and I began accepting his words incredibly but acted as if I am not!

Winding this topic, Renuka hugging me said good night and left my place.

Then turned our conversation on,

"So what is a crush?" I asked.

"Crush! crush!! um! crush that's it!" he said.

"So can I tell you, crush is an emotion of love on the person you don't know much."

"Yeah, this one," he said.

"Too childish you are, what was your intension of me, being your crush?" I asked.

"I want you to speak to me all these four years of the voyage, and once if you get committed with some other, I'll surely skip everything and would not enable myself to be in touch with you," these were his words.

Hearkening to this, I don't know what, but I am truly disgruntled.

From that day, he initiated calling me CRUSH.

He once said with his broad heart open that,

"CRUSH,

I'll never admit you down with my words or litigations. No matter what, and how absurd you behave, I'll never get irritated with you. Trust me, I relish all your trials. I don't just like you, furthermore, I like every act you do because YOU are implicated in that."

Listening that, I was leasing wings from pigeon to drift high into the atmosphere.

I insisted on him, "I am short-tempered and you existing so patience cannot proceed your journey of four years with me and I maintain a lot of attitudes."

"Actually I am short-tempered, but to you, I am not! Even I maintain more attitude than you, I never texted someone first. I never begged someone sorry. Nevertheless, it is barely for you I smash my barricades of attitude," his words softened me.

My inner voice said, "Hey idiot! stop being so sweet to me, I may get addicted to you!"

It was one evening that I have flooded with the messages from the groups on WhatsApp which made me neglect him. I could not answer him promptly as I have to swap between WhatsApp and Instagram. He then asked if I was busy, I said to him that it was getting hard for me to switch between two different apps and inquired if he would mind joining me on WhatsApp so that I would handily text. He said okay.

798163252, you can now join me.*

Very next moment, he texted, "Hai."

With this simple Hai, the journey on WhatsApp made us know additional and explore uniquely.

"Hey, what did you save my contact?"

"Guess!" he said.

"Crush?" I threw a stone in dark.

"You are too close, Crush. But it is CANDY CRUSH that I saved your contact, and what about mine in yours?"

"It is RAM that I saved, but now, it's gonna change."

"And what is that?" he questioned.

"If I am your CRUSH, you will be CANDY on my phone. We together make Candy Crush," I said with two smirking emojis.

"By the way, do you like it?" I asked for his opinion.

"I already said you, I like everything about you and whatever label you give me, I respond the way you like," he said.

He would not notice, but I am blushing in!

We became very attached as if, we neither started nor ended our day without each other's text.

It was 10:30 that night, I got everything done by that time and switched my data ON, I found his notification on the top.

"Hey! had dinner?" he asked.

"No, and what about you?" I answered.

With no reply to my question, "Why did you skip dinner tonight?" he interrogated.

"I am not interested in the menu, Candy. So I didn't!" I responded.

"Crush, if you aren't interested in the menu, go with some curd rice. I seriously plead you, please don't skip your meal," he begged.

"I don't even like curd but stuffed some snacks in the canteen and I'll not skip anymore," I fibbed.

"Crush, tell me what all you like?" he initiated.

"I like Virat Kohli, I even like Surya, I like Bhuvneswar Kumar, Kane Williamson, Chris Woakes, ABD."

"Crush Crush….! Are you a cricket buzz?" he interrupted my list.

"Yeah, Candy. I adore cricket," I rejoined.

"Okay then, carry on with your list," he resumed.

"Hahaha, now you tell me who do you like?" I posed the same question.

"I like you crush," he said.

"Aaaree Candy, I'm asking about the celebrities," I texted slamming my head.

"I am a huge fan of Virat Kohli so is my Instagram ID, ram_virat. By the way, all those you mentioned are my favorites too," he answered.

"Leave about me and continue yours," he said.

"What else do you wish to know?" I extended.

"Your interests and likes," he added.

"I am interested in sports, reading novels, I like black and white colors, number 3, I crave for custard apple, non-veg, chocolates," I paused as he interrupted.

"What is your favorite chocolate?" he asked.

"Whatever it may be, but if it is chocolate, I lick my lips. Among all those, KitKat is my favorite," I added.

"Hey Crush, even I love KitKat," he said elatedly.

"Asking that if anyone proposed you is a fatal crime and rather, how many would be the valid substitute, how many proposed you?" he asked.

"NO ONE!" I pranked.

"Listen to me, I will not adore girls so easily. I complain about every sort of aspect but I liked you wholeheartedly, that implies you would have a very huge line of

followers waiting for your approval, please tell me about them," he persuaded.

"What will you do with all those stories?" I asked.

"Even I should know how competitive the world is, right ?" he countered with a winking emoji.

I said to him about Arvind, the one who has been trying me from my grade five. A guy who proposed me in grade five. And one who told me about his love on the very final day of my tenth-grade board examinations, another one who followed me on the bus and was even beaten up by Arvind, the additional was my junior who was a victim of hurts from Arvindh for liking me. A senior from my academy. My friend's brother proposed to me on Valentine's day in PUC. A senior in this college said that I am his crush and followed me wherever I go. Another one from the same year, as the senior fell for me at the very first sight. My 10th classmate recently said that he was crushing on me.

"Crush! please hold on, I think you will take the entire dark to give your list. And I wonder if this is considered NO ONE !" he interrupted and then exclaimed.

"Now you tell me, how many proposals you encountered?" I questioned him.

"A girl proposed me on WhatsApp and I blocked her, a junior attempted compiling my details as she likes me, and… that's it, not a long list like yours," he admitted.

"What about Praveenya?" I asked with a massive apprehension.

He held his breathe tight and started, "So, she requested me on Facebook and I accepted her. She used to text day-to-day and one day she proposed to me. I said her NO. From that day, people began stimulating a rumor that I admired Praveenya and she too adored me but that isn't true," he said.

"Then why didn't you attempt warning people about the truth?" I texted.

"Crush, She is a girl, once she gets an imputation, it would not be fixed right though she tries. And I would not mind taking up the burden for redeeming her. Even I too have a sister," he sounded quite diplomatic.

This truly made me alter my attitude, my perception, and took my feelings to another level. Listening to all these, respect towards him stroked the clear sky and had no qualm.

"Can I ask you something?" I inquired if I could ask. I know, he never said NO.

As predicted, he asked me to proceed.

"What do you like in me?" solicited with a curious mind.

"No, I cannot just tell you, please don't ask me Crush. In fact, I am not sure what I all I love," he halted my curiosity.

"Please tell me, Candy. Please!" I wished.

"Crush! listen, you should never plead someone nor ask sorry. By the way, don't ever convey to me sorry or thank you. Let me tell you something, in the very first moment I saw, I didn't feel like you are that gorgeous nor I didn't think I will fall for you, but as I saw you the next day, the day after and the following days, I could not take my eyes off," he ended.

I gave a nonchalant response and closed the chat though I was dancing in.

IDEAL HUSBAND QUALITIES

It was Saturday dawn. I had a weekend shuffle planned at the noon by the administration. I here was, all the computer science students. And once we are done, the Mechanical students followed. By the way, Ram is from the Mighty Mech! As we were scheduled at noon, I didn't hurry bathing or scrubbing my teeth but was swamped on Instagram. Parnika and Nila had a gaze on me, the way I grinned in between the conversation and they cackled like the sound would blast someone's eardrum. They were just asking me who was on the other side of my smiles. I just didn't even deem their words and was altering my moods by conversing.

They commented, "The other side of the chat could not see all your expressions and they may go in vain buddy. By the way, when are you going to introduce our brother?"

"Hey, he is just my friend!" I cleared.

So, is the discussion going in the room and I had my chat on Instagram.

He asked, "Hey Crush, what fascinates you about a boy, and how do you want a perfect boy to be?"

"You know what, Candy, I get attracted to boys in a black shirt with his sleeves cuffed till elbows and light blue denim to it," I explained.

"Still?" he said wanting something supplementary.

"He should be tall and decent with a sharp nose and lamp brown eyes that will kill me all my way. Anyways, I have several qualities that are to be embedded," I elongated.

"What are they, Crush? Tell me please," he asked me with curiosity.

"There is a list of some ideal husband qualities that I wrote a long back and discovering a guy with all those personalities is a bit difficult," I added.

"Tell me those qualities and I'll judge if it is tough or easy," he said.

I sent him an image which had some script written in my handwriting.

The heading comes, IDEAL HUSBAND QUALITIES.

The sheet was adorned with many emojis having love symbols in their eyes of varied sizes and drawn with different colors all over.

1. The first and foremost thing is, he should be approved by my papa.

2. He should take care of my parents as his ones.

3. He should be a complete dear with no guilty addictions.

4. He should have zero anger and ego.

5. He should have a smiling face all the time.

6. Like every girl dreams, he should be handsome.

7. Moreover, he should propose directly with a white tulip.

"Am I sounding bizarre?" I asked.

"Just a bit. I didn't hear someone writing so," he stated.

"Not every girl can take chance in her proceedings but it is only imagination where she is not restricted. I wanted my life partner to be so," I said.

"Yeah, there are no bounds for imagination but one gets comfortable when their intuitions come true. And it isn't a big deal for those to befall in your case," he added.

"But finding a white tulip is one of the biggest tasks and before that, I should like him right?" I tuned.

"Yeah, this might be one of the toughest tasks," he admitted.

"And what all you hate in a boy?" he questioned.

"I loathe if boys use some beaded chains, bracelets, crocs, and pertain tint to their strands," I concluded.

"And what qualities do you desire to marry?" I posed the question.

"She should have long hair, should keep up peace in the populace and make hell in the room and…! she should be…..she should be….just the way YOU are! And I have no other words to describe my girl," he responded.

"Okay then, I'll search a Rapunzel for you," I added.

"Hey, Crush! Did I ask you to search for someone? It's okay if you don't even have long hair. I admire the way you are," he stated his opinion.

"By the way, prepared for the weekend?" I inquired distracting the topic.

"I hate weekends as I cannot see you!" he expressed himself.

"Don't you feel it's getting too much?" I raised.

"You never trusted me and I cannot help!" he said.

"Hahaha, okay then I'll fresh up and prepare for the weekend," I concluded.

"Okay, but Crush, text me when you are done with your exam so that I can be a bit early and pass by you!" he told.

"Sure sure Candy, bye!" I ended smiling.

I then stepped out of my bed. I made my bones set right in their places bending forward, then backward, later both the sides alternatively. Next made my wrist into its position and wished both my roomies, A VERY HAPPY MORNING stretching my hands high. They smiled and asked me to brush and bath so that I would have some time to prepare myself for the weekend. I went to the washroom with my clothes and towel to take a shower. Later got ready in my college uniform and began my preparation.

I started with OOPS. Even God would not have an idea of how many bullets pierced my body while I was studying this. Every chapter was like a missile and this subject drenched me with extensive fear. Somehow reached ashore in it. Next was DBMS, it was a piece of cake and it didn't trouble me much because I perfectly listened to the topic and made running notes too. I liked the way my lecturer conveyed the lecture. I finished it just like the rabbit winning the running race. One after the other, I made all the subjects reach to an end and started to mess.

I got strict instruction from Candy to take curd as a part of my lunch just because it neutralizes my body as I intake a lot of spicy food. He is fond of curd and I run away from it. I had lunch and Sathwika joined me in mess and she even got the same classroom as I did. So, we headed towards the allocated room with our laptop, a pen, and a paper as it is a multiple-choice online examination. After five minutes of our presence in the class, started our test. Exam being a multiple choice type, we were a bit confident about our result but to our surprise, all those four options seemed quite similar. Somehow, we managed to complete. I stepped out and switched my mobile on.

"Candy, I am done and where are you?" I asked.

"I am on my way, Crush. I'll be there in ten minutes," he said.

Meanwhile, Sathwika asked me to join her towards the dormitory.

I said, "Parnika needs a laptop as her system had a backup problem and she will come here to collect. I will have to wait for her."

The reason I said to her was true but the place we were waiting at isn't! The destination was damn far from the place we were at. For every two minutes, Sathwika reminded Parnika and started boosting for the delay in her presence.

"Candy! where are you?" I inquired.

"I am near the turning point and you?" he said.

"I am at the ending of the turning," I replied.

I made myself ready to face him. I was checking if everything was all right with me. Then came, Candy! adjusting his silky hair to one of the sides as he always did. I saw him and he even did. It wasn't a countable period he saw. It was neither negligible, as he saw, he turned his face. I wondered, what's wrong with him and commenced to my dormitory.

Then I texted,

"You are too bad at utilizing opportunity, Candy," I pitied him.

"Crush, it is really hard for me to face when you are peeking at me. I cannot even dare to maintain eye contact with you. But trust me, I can stay the whole day long watching you from a distance," he gave a lengthy explanation.

"Okay then, I am leaving. Best of luck, do well," I wished.

"Yeah thank you, please go safe. I'll text you once I complete my test," he intimated.

On my way, I found Parnika, I handed my laptop to her and went to the room with Sathwika. I set everything for an elegance nap instantly after our stretch. I have a decent relationship with my bed. It was a drug for my grief and emphasis. I charged my mobile and hit the sack at 4:00 p.m.

Parnika woke me up, I unlocked my mobile. It was 7:30 p.m, I along with my roommates got prepared to mess, had dinner, and came back. Then, I checked for notifications, they were around ten messages from a single contact and it was from him!

Crush,

I am done with my exam, what are you doing?

Hello!!!

Are you there!? Crush?

Two weeping emojis

Had something, chocolate at least?

Reply please, followed by a GIF confiding me that he was waiting.

Are you asleep?

Crush…Even I am sleeping. What can I do online without you?!

Last call…Are you there?

Okay then…Text me after you wake up.

Bye.

After reading this, I was laughing for his childishness. But felt sorry too.

"Hey Candy!" I initiated the chat.

"Crush! where have you gone? I was just waiting like anything here," he exploded with grief.

"I am sorry, Candy. I fell asleep and could not respond," I apologized.

"I said you not to apologize. What is this again?" he said.

"Made you wait for a longer time?" I asked.

"Yeah, but no worry, I liked waiting. You know what Crush, I tapped in for every notification that I got and checked if it is yours," he told.

"Hmph…okay then, from today, I will let you know a bit early if I am busy," I compensated.

"This is much better," he agreed.

"So, can I ask you something?"

"You are always free to ask me anything," he said.

"Did you ever hated me in this period of the journey?" I texted him this way.

"I liked you passionately and how would you expect me to hate you!?" he answered.

"At some sort of time, we even hate those we are fond of. I hope that happened with me too. Mention that moment," I extended.

"I hate you in two moments, one is when you cry, and second is when you suffocate sitting in the last row of your classroom and sweat like anything," he claimed.

"What will you do if I come near you crying?" I triggered him with this question.

"I will close my eyes Crush! Seriously, I will close my eyes first. Once you stop crying, I'll ask you what's the matter?" he exploded and I was like !!!!

"I can't even imagine you weeping, Crush and I don't even wish to get that day!" he concluded.

GOWTHAM - A PAIN IN THE NECK

It was around 2:30 a.m, my eyes grew tired but my heart was still active. I became absorbed, oblivious to the passage of time. I was texting him on Instagram.

"Till date, you have been comprehending me, right? Today, at any cost, I'll be knowing you and you will have to tell me, okay?" I asked.

"You are my crush, so I have to know you and it is mandatory. But, you knowing me, is of no intention," he countered.

"You are my friend and getting aware about my friend is also considered compulsory," I locked.

"Tell me what do you need?" he asked.

"Whom do you converse on social media, I mean only girls?" I questioned.

"You, my sister and Rishitha, she is from my townlet," he said.

He once said that a girl proposed him on WhatsApp. I assumed she is Rishitha and began taunting him but the result was out to be an erroneous assumption.

"Give me Rishitha's contact, I will talk to her," I pleaded.

"But for what?" he asked.

"Give me, Candy," I said.

He sent me her number. I said that I'll call her in the morning. Before I make a hash of the situation,

He said, "Hey I'll inform her about you. I got that you are trying to make something worse."

"What will you say?" I asked.

"I like you and you are my crush," he texted.

"Okay, go convey her," I said in a very absurd way.

"I am serious, Crush. I'll surely say her and I am not credible for anything," he cleared.

"Haa, okay okay," I perpetrated with a confidence that he wouldn't.

"Okay then, I'll text her now so that she will see in the morning," he told.

"Please proceed," I replied.

A girl gonna call you tomorrow and I like her she is my crush. Please don't mind her words.

He texted her this way and sent me a screenshot.

"Hey Candy, did you send or are you just tricking me?" I asked with a lot of anxiety.

"I sent it Crush!" he responded.

"Hey, delete it. I was just jesting and didn't think you would send," I said it worrying.

"Yeah, I'll do it. Give me a second," he asked.

I was then able to sniff and was waiting for his message.

"Are you done?" I asked.

"Crush! An omission and I'm so sorry!" he fretted.

Before I could ask him, he said that,

"I, in hurry deleted it FOR ME," he said.

"Aah! What shall we do now?" I terrified.

"There is nothing left to do, let's wait for the consequences," he answered.

"It's all my mistake, I have not asked you to message her! The fault is all mine," I admitted.

"No worries. I'll speak to her in the morning, don't panic. I'll plead her not to spread it and she is a trustworthy girl," he consoled.

Then, we were out of the topic and speaking about some other things and in between,

"Crush, will you send me one of your pics?" he asked.

"I am sorry. I usually do not send my pictures to boys. I even hide my status to all my male peers. Please don't mind me!" I refused so softly.

"One at least?" he pleaded.

"You do have a sister and if someone asks her in this way, will she grant?" I disputed with a question.

He said, "That's okay", and didn't text me any further.

"One day, I'll surely give you," I complimented.

"Candy, it has been three years you were watching me but I didn't notice you at any moment," I said diverting the topic.

"I saw you very clearly when you came for an announcement to our class and found you hiding from GOWTHAM. I thought you noticed me that day," he replied.

"How come you know about Gowtham?!" I asked in aghast.

GOWTHAM…! A character that I have to speak of. It was all those days after my examinations in PUC 2. I got an unknown request on Instagram. The account was read, *_gowtham_*. I deleted it, as I don't know him. It was a public account. I found some of his pictures posted. He looked quite decent, tall with a pair of frameless glasses, some of the facial hair grown, his mustache and beardy face looked attractive. I checked for his followers and following.

I came to know that he was from our college and he followed Karthik on Instagram. But, I haven't heard his name till date nor saw him. He again requested I canceled it. Hope this happened two to three times. Then came the text in the inbox. In the very beginning, he texted excessively natural and as it turned more, he began extolling. He praised me as no one did! It did not make me fly because it was all unreal. His words were like, no other girl in this world looks better than me! I was damn fed and ordered him to end this nonsense.

I, then called Karthik and asked him if he knows Gowtham, as Karthik was followed by him. He said that he knew him and asked if there was any problem with that guy. I said that he was flirting. Karthik then asked me if he could warn him. I replied that there is no issue to worry but just extolling and, if something goes wrong, I would block him. He asked me to take care and ended the call.

One day, an incident befell so that, I removed my Instagram account. I got some texts from an account with my profile and ID. The texts were so bad that a girl wouldn't read. So, I was upset that day. They continued to send the same messages with my ID and profile to some of my school friends. Somehow, with the help of my brother, Pradeep, it got solved and the fake account got deleted. I was glad to see the back of him as I got a conclusion to Gowtham's chapter with an end to Instagram.

But, it drove him to text me on WhatsApp. One fine day, he proposed to me. I said I didn't have any opinion of liking a guy at this moment and denied. Even after rejecting, he didn't choose another way. He messaged me on Whatsapp, I didn't respond to any of his messages. I blocked him but he came up with the other numbers to contact. I said to him so clear that I am not at all interested. He was a pain in the neck. After so long time, I came to know that, he isn't just loving me, in addition to it, flirting many other girls on social media.

I gave him many threats through text messages, he didn't consider any of them. He followed wherever I go, he told all his friends about me. They abetted him and started chanting his name wherever they found me. It was such a predicament. He used to urge all my peers about my doings and waited near my classroom to watch me. Though he cared, it always seemed disingenuous.

To my question, "He is my PUC classmate and a very close friend to me, he knew that I admired you and I used to tell him all my stories about you. I didn't expect him to feel like the way I did," Ram answered.

I then thought,

If your crush is loved by someone, it is not he or she but you who have to be blamed for, because, the way you described, made him fall for her!

And for GOWTHAM'S chapter, it was RAM who have to be blamed for!

HARSHITH - MY CRUSH

The following morn, I texted Rishitha and conversed about him. She was inquiring about the subject between Ram and me. I said that he was just crushing and nothing deeper. We had a submissive talk and wanted to see each other. So that Monday morning, I pinged her through the phone. She urged me to come to one of the edges of the block that we were staying in. So, our blocks were built in such a way that, if we stand at one of the sides, we can have a view of another block that is adjacent to it. I came to the corner of our building and she even did.

I saw her, she is fair enough, a bit taller to me, she had wavy hair with curls in the caps, besides, she is pretty. We had a girly discussion over the phone for some time and dropped the call. Then, I got ready in my college uniform and commenced to class. That day, by the time I reached, it was more than half of the class that got occupied. Anyhow, I got a place in the second row next to Sathwika. Sitting in the second row was a little profitable.

Is it for you!? No! It's for Candy. Because it is the only row that was apparent to those who pass by our class opening. And it was Candy, who always holds for my presence in the classroom. Every time he observes me, he would text, "Crush, I saw you" with two loving emojis. As usual, he saw me and texted.

That day, after finishing lunch, I convened in my classroom, he texted me so,

"Hey, you remained near the common water point for about two minutes, then brought two water bottles, filled one by one, later, you sipped some water from the green bottle and loaded the incompleteness. And started back to your classroom. All my worry is why did you carry both the bottles while your friend is leading with empty hands. You would have given one!"

"Candy! Were you near the water point at that moment?" I asked surprisingly.

"Yeah, I was welcoming some pleasure watching you," he said passionately.

"Crush, I even heeded you to an extent. You have very clear and snowy feet with black nail polish on your nails!" he exclaimed.

"Hahaha, by the way, where are you now?" I asked.

"I am exactly contrary to you near class 5. I saw you till now, what are you articulating to your friend for so long time?" he questioned.

So, before I could notice him, he went to his class. Then,

I texted him, "I don't know but I make endless chirp and don't even feel like making an effort in conversing nor expect some rest."

"Conceal some for future," he joked.

As the class started, I zipped my bag with my mobile in and listened to the class. It was English hour, the only class I wait for. I wish to add something to my bio. I love JAM sessions and debates and would contribute an energetic role in all the activities in this hour and perpetually had a very positive response with my communication in class. So, with all the exercises for that day, we ended taking up the assignment. I stuffed my bag and headed towards my dorm along with Sathwika. It was his message on Whatsapp,

"Hai crush," said he.

"Hey hai, what are you up to?" I asked.

So, we had a blunt conversation. I swiftly asked him to send me the screenshot of my chat.

He sent me, I was about to check his wallpaper. But I found my contact saved as 1807201937.

"Hey what is this? Why is my contact saved with some random numbers?" I disputed.

"It isn't a random number. It owns some meaning," he said.

"Meaning! what is that?" I asked with enthusiasm.

"18/07/2019 is the date of my first text to you. Then, 3 is your favorite number, 7 is mine and so is your contact 1807201937," he explained.

"Superb! I should proffer a bow to your creativity," I praised. "And to beautify it and make it look like a contact number, add '96' in front, one of the feel-good movies," I stated.

"I wish to have some crisp of craziness in all my deeds," he responded.

"Even I will save your contact number in this format with precise fittings, 91807193718. 18/07/19 is the offset of our journey, 3 is my favorite, and 7 is yours, 9 in the prefix is just to embellish. Finally, 18 is our VIRAT's jersey number," I said.

"Woah Crush!" he elated.

"I had a doubt streaming in my mind for so long time. I don't admire myself, I wonder how you fancied me?" I asked.

"You don't like YOU! Okay then, I'll sow a seed of love in you," he said.

"What?!" I exclaimed.

"I mean, I'll sow a seed of love to love yourself in you," he elongated.

"Let's see," I said.

"So, I heard that you will not speak to girls for a sustained period," I inquired.

"Yeah, I don't know why but, I discontinue the talk promptly. I never spoke to a girl for more than three months," he stated.

"Is that!?" I exclaimed.

"But, I wish this would not happen with you," he told.

"Hahaha, hoping so," I said smiling.

"I have to fresh up and start my work for today. I'm leaving," I said.

And he even said the same and ended the conversation. The time then was proximately 7:00 p.m.

I took a refreshing shower and then, dressed up in my favorite black t-shirt and pink checked pair of shorts. I initiated the Design and Analysis of Algorithms (DAA) Assignment that I have to submit the next day. I started drawing my N Queen problem and state-space trees. I liked this subject and the one who teaches it too. My DAA lecturer is pretty friendly and more expressive. I could easily grasp her words and did an erudite work in her class. Somehow I achieved my task and switched to OOPS Observation. As every Engineering student is much familiar and more habituated to CTRL X and CTRL

V in records and observations. Even, I obeyed the same law instead of inscribing it on my own.

I made it impeccable by 8:00 p.m. I know I would skip dinner, so is my dressing. I would not continuously work for longspun. So, I relocated to WhatsApp. I was viewing one of my friends WhatsApp status, it was a feel-good song performed by a Youtuber and he did a marvelous job in stealing my heart. I watched it again, another time, one more time and by the time I ended, it was 37th turn for the video to play. I began to crush on him and became a staunch fan. I watched almost all his videos. Every time I viewed, he made me fall for his eloquence, his attitude, his voice whatnot.

I got to know that he is Harshith Reddy from Hyderabad and was pursuing his BTech second year in the same department as mine. I was somewhere around heaven knowing that he was a year senior to me and from the same department. These two statements resonated in my ears and I was reddening. I was lost in his thoughts and didn't bother what's happening in and around me.

"Hey Candy, watch this," I sent the video with loving emojis followed.

After two long minutes, "Who is that guy?" he asked.

"He is my CRUSH!, Candy," I replied with a lot of zeal.

"WHAT!?" he reacted very immediately.

"Yeah, I just saw him and was seriously crushing," I explained my curiosity.

"What are you speaking, Crush?! First, tell me who the hell is he?" he questioned out of anger.

"He is a Youtuber from Hyderabad. He is pursuing his BTech second year that means he is a year senior to me. Moreover, he is from my department," I pulled his leg saying this.

"Thank god! He was a Youtube star?" he said with his tension off.

From that day, I started chorusing Harshith's name near him. He became mad and asked me to stop saying his name. He was jealous! I liked that possessiveness and made a lot of fun practicing that name. My craze towards him erupted like a Volcano. Our chat was quite peculiar with his entrance.

"Hey Crush, what's up?" he asked.

"I just had a conversation with Harshith," I said just to bake jealous in him.

"Harshith! Harshith! Don't you have another topic to say?" he frowned.

"Okay then, what's going on?" I questioned.

"I just completed my assignment," he answered.

"Oh, you know what Candy, CSE, and CSE makes the best pair. It's going to be proved. I mean to say about Harshith," I said exhilarated.

"Who said it is CSE and CSE? A Mechanical boy and CSE girl makes the best pair and it is a universal fact," he argued.

"So now, I have to search for a guy from Mechanical!" I said with a load of smileys.

"Crush, I am from the Mechanical. Fine, you will never understand me," he added.

I laughed striking his words though I knew his intension.

We always started our conversation on WhatsApp and ended it on Instagram. The only reason is, staying on WhatsApp for a prolonged interval makes people see my presence notified by an ONLINE alert. So, I would never let people know that I am online. Once the clock strikes 10:00 p.m, we would switch to Instagram. This happened daily. It is not just one or two, there were days where we chatted till 3 in the morning and wake up as usual and attended our classes. I still wonder what we had in our chat!

The insane habit we both had was, as the clock ticks midnight, the one who wishes GOOD MORNING will be the winner for that day. There was no sort of punishment to the looser nor reward given to the winner but just a trivial act. It's all the three we covered, WhatsApp, Instagram, and offline message. If he is first on Instagram and offline message, I would be on WhatsApp and vice versa. Sometimes, it would end in a tie and we had no tiebreaker and extended our smiles for our irrational acts.

DID I FALL FOR HIM?

I never forgot the day I saw her,

It was her pretty feet striding towards me!

Her expressive eyes hunting for her peers.

I expected her attention would have a pause at me.

I could feel the glitter in her eyes,

that made me fall for her.

She! clearing her silky hair and adjusting it slowly back at her ears,

I'm grateful for breeze just because

it gave me such an amazing view to watch.

Her smile, that cute one, literally collapsed me all my way!

Her tiny lips were restless, the constant chirp she made was effortless.

I wish she would have concealed some for the future!

Finally, her innocent face, mischievous acts, and sweet words were adorable,

Waiting! waiting ! for ME to fall in her glance !!

I just penned this down. I didn't just put it down for one's sake but enjoyed comprehending kinda stuff and few from my own experience too!

And then, it was 4:00 in the dusk, we were invited to attend the auditorium to witness the inauguration of TeCRUSH 2k19, a technical fest that is celebrated in our institute. We were getting ready to attend. He then asked,

"Crush, Are you coming to the auditorium?"

"Yeah, I am on my way," I replied.

"What about you?" I asked.

"I am waiting here" he asserted.

"Is that?!" I said making a mockery.

"Yeah, what will Candy do without Crush here?" he added.

"Fine, fine, you are excelling in poetry these days!" I claimed.

"I know that you won't believe me. Anyways, come fast," he said.

I replied to him with my entrance. I perched in one of the back rows of the left corner. He acknowledged to me everything, the way I entered, hunted for a place, and got settled. The program was on and we were texting each other wonted. Then came a group on to the dais for a dance feat. And Praveenya was one of those particular groups. As she strode on the stage, I started texting him about her and chimed her name. He became mad at me but I didn't stop.

"Candy, can I yell your name?" I asked with a winking emoji.

"Shut up! Stop it, Crush, please," he almost begged.

Somehow, I bluffed to put a verge but initiated furthermore. He was like slamming his skull. We didn't follow the program, rather chatted, and he could see me from the place where he was and notified every doings of mine. He said that he wanted to have more and more fests and programs so that he would gawk me! I was just chuckling for his words. We got loosened with the event but ahead was the actual hardship where we have to take down our mid terminals.

Days were running like an express. We were almost in the midway of our semester. And left out with two more days to give a try to second mid assessments. And my heart was pumping extra liter blood as it does for every sort of terminal exams. I made a timetable set for my preparation. I had five subjects to study. Among them, one subject carries two credits, and all other subjects pack four. So, I focused more on those high credit subjects and a bit less on scoring the left out ones. As I have two days in my hands, I planned to complete two subjects per day and the other subject on the day of the exam.

Our mid terminals were scheduled in two days and we were deemed to write two subjects on a day, one in the morning and the other at noon. Other three on the next day in the same pattern but one in the morning and two in the afternoon. We didn't speak much in the exam time but we would wish good morning and good night, as I said, we neither started nor ended the day without texting each other.

As Parnika was from the Mechanical, she would tell me the important topics that were to be covered for the mid and I used to give him the list. He was almost done by the time I gave. He focused on the last two assessments and didn't bother much writing the first one. We always thought we would surely fail if we continue to chat like this. I don't still understand why I am that attached to this man!

So, I am almost done with the task that I have planned for that day and even left out with many hours. I was watching some Instagram feed. Then, I was interrupted by a mail from the administration providing us with the shuffle for the exams. It was some 50kb file that I have downloaded. The very first ID number that I searched was mine, S360223.

I was placed in the Gama cluster, room number four, third row, fourth place. We were accommodated in a few clusters named Kappa, Lambda, Omega, Mue, Gama, Eta, Sigma, Alpha during our class hours. I checked for the people next to me both right and left, then back and front. The very next search was his ID number, S360510. As he ever hoped to be in the same class as mine but his expectation would never satisfy him and even this time, he was placed in Kappa cluster, room number eight, fourth row, first place.

As I examined mine, I looked over for his adjacent people. To both sides and front were some random male ones from his department. And the back was that girl whom I didn't think that I would hate much. She was Praveenya. Subsequently, watching her name next to him, gallons of blood were moving vigorously into one single vein.

I was so suffocated and mad but whom shall I show this on! Who would endorse my anger? Hold on! Why are you angry and what for? My inner voice asked. I have no answer for this. I asked myself, why am I angry? My internal speech again raised, Is that because you aren't in her place? or Are you jealous that she was in a place in which you were supposed and expected to be?

I questioned myself, Am I jealous of her, being with him? If so, why am I? Do I like him? Am I crushing on him the way he was? What if I like him? My questions were endless and very continuous. I broke all these, clearing my internal monologue that, the place he was allocated is not my cup of tea, so I didn't like the shuffle. That instant, I was like, if someone vexed me, I would have severely smacked across their face and it's like a red rag to a bull. To his misfortune, he texted me that moment,

"Hey, hai."

"What are you doing?"

I didn't reply to him, then came his text, "BUSY?", that gave scope for me to spew my anger on him. And started...

"Yeah, I know who the hell is busy with their classmates."

"What's wrong with you Midhuna?"

"Nothing like that, you are busy with your beloved. I am so sorry to disturb you," I was scowling.

"Whom are you talking about and have you gone mad or what? Why are you so silly?" he asked in chaos.

"Yeah, I am mad. I expected, someday you would say this. Fine, it's me, the idiotic girl," I was replying in a frown.

"Crush, don't take my words seriously, I am just telling you, that's it," he tried to clear everything.

"Fine, I was mad a minute ago, and now I am a joke. As you wish, go with all the creepy descriptions. Anyway, I would accept anything so easy and you never treated me earnestly. Joking on people doesn't fetch you something, Candy!" I added almost puking my anger.

"I didn't mean so! What happened to you? I never treated you a joke," he said with a lot of patience.

"Will you please stop it, I came to know everything. Are you expecting something to happen or disappointed that nothing happened?" locked him with my senseless reply.

"My God! my intension isn't that. Where did we start and where are you taking it?" he asked.

"Nothing!" I said reluctantly.

"First tell me, what is the reason behind this talk?" he said very pleasingly.

"Shall I catch you up later, I am not in a mood to chat," I stated.

"Sure, but take care," he concerned.

I didn't reply anything and closed the chat.

We didn't speak properly for two days, and the first day of our mid passed in that period. He texted every while albeit I wasn't giving a proper reply. So poor man he was, I was pitying for sternly telling him off. Why would I show my anger or my own jealous on him with no mistake of his's? Concealing all my annoyance, I texted him as usual and he was over the moon. He asked me the cause of my weird behavior. I enclosed his words with some arbitrary reason. He was laughing at my sayings. And we were just the same as earlier. We completed our mid terminals and were happy enjoying the weekend texting each other.

By the end, he thought I threw him into turmoil but it was vice versa. I wonder why, I am that possessive towards him. Did I fall for him?!

But then, I knew,

Possessiveness is not always LOVE,

We can even possess the things we like,

And there is a lot of difference between love and like!

TECRUSH DAY 1

We got a hectic schedule and were dead on our feet. The only point I fret about is a dearth of enjoyment. The same old story, observations, records, labs, internals, externals, mids, and semesters we had! I needed a tranquil day to repose very badly. Soon after the accomplishment of our mid terminals, our clusters were swamped, we could find clubs of people in hurry, some roaming here and there with papers in their hands, few sketching something just like event planners, and a group of 5 students visiting each class for an announcement. What is the message about? We were giving thought to the brain and discovered that it was all regarding "TECRUSH", our technical fest. Technical or non-technical, we naturally make it cultural. My heart reposed knowing that we were going to have a whale of a time.

Eventually, that mass attained our class and we were moved to listen to the events they come up with. They sprang with around 6-7 branch events and ended with some open to all events. They concluded saying us to utilize the opportunity and register as many games as possible. Some of my classmates were triggering them with questions and others with senseless talk.

The wait has come to an end. We were now left out with two more days, the registrations attained the zenith, all the volunteers bunked the classes to decorate the campus, few were involved organizing the program and we were making hell in the classrooms as the lectures weren't fully on. I registered for a few events and the registration fee was pretty affordable. Once we pay fifty rupees, we have access to enroll for all the contests possible. Even the promotions were rather fast and registrations were being done in our dormitories too. That day, in the duskiness, after I came from the shower, I was asking him,

"Did you register for TECRUSH?"

"No! I am not much excited to participate," he answered.

"Not excited in the sense? Wish to linger like this the whole college life without being exposed to the world?"

"Don't spring the philosophical dialogues now, Crush," he said.

"I don't know what, but I am enrolling you now, right at the instant," I stated.

"Hey yar, please don't do that!" he pleaded.

I came out of the chat and called one of my friends who was holding up registrations. I asked if she was free so that, I could go and record him for the fest.

She said she was unoccupied and I went and requested her to give me the lappy so that I can directly enter his details and password. She proffered me as she was one of my close friends. To join, we need an ID number and contact number of the entry. S360510, *897884924 were his details and Ram18 was set as his password. **The registration was successful** the screen was noting this and I captured it on my mobile and sent him.

I paid for her online and left the room thanking.

"You made it?!" he replied with shocking emojis.

"Now if you don't engage, I will mark your end."

"Okay okay."

"Donno who named the event, but it is all for my pleasure T CRUSH," he blushed pausing at crush.

"Hahaha, as people advertised the event name, the very first thought I got is you," I said.

I then got a notification from phone pey, Ram sent you 100 rupees. I was furious noticing that. I instantly transferred him and texted on WhatsApp.

"Hey, monkey! Why did you transfer 100 rupees?"

"You recorded me right?" he replied.

"So what? By the way mister, I won't accept payment from my friends."

"Even I won't, but you aren't my friend. You are my Crush as I informed you beforehand," he countered.

"Whatever, if you return me, I am certain that I would ever articulate you again," I said.

He said okay and our topic veered somewhither.

Tomorrow is TeCRUSH and today evening is like a hustling town. ECE students were assigned a task to renovate their classrooms and the champ will be declared on the day of the fest by the faculty members as the inspectors. So they were indeed busy just like the bees. And I along with Parnika went to mess and we wanted to while away the haptic due, having a look at the fest and the classroom decorations. We headed to the ECE cluster, my eyes glittered!

Classrooms were shipshape, transparently mopped, tables and chairs were tidy and arranged skillfully, colorful papers were cut so professional into fascinating shapes and fixed throughout the classroom, some of them hanging in between, the walls were perfectly designed with their department logos, there were few quotes stuck high above the head level. Ultimately entrance, the door got everything that it can depict the class. Not just a single room but every room got its creativity and students who contributed were stamped talented. All those beatifications brought out pre-event celebrations. With that, we averted ourselves to our room. I was too early to bed that day and too late to wake up the next daylight.

I could detect people getting set to visit the project expo. I considered my sleep more prominent than anything else at that moment. After a notably long time, I sensed someone thumping at my door. Is that pleasing? I always seemed like hitting them hard but once I come out of my utopia, I love them for doing the right thing. Yet those sounds were getting on my nerves.

Parnika opened, it was Renuka who appeared to wake me up and was half dead accomplishing it. Lastly, I awoke and she pleaded me to come to the project expo. And stated that, she may not be accessible to company me as she was running early to exhibit her project. I said I'll be there by noon and yawned again. She was ecstatic that I'm somehow coming. I woke up at 11:30 almost at noon.

"Hey Crush, where are you?" he texted.

"Just woke up, still on my bed," I replied.

"Is that! I assumed you were somewhere near the expo and I was exploring. When are you coming?" he asked.

"I'll be there by noon."

"Please come fast, I'll remain till you come."

"For?!" I asked as if I don't know anything with laughing smileys.

"Just to see you maa!" he replied with face-palm emojis.

"Hahaha, fine. I'll text you soon after my arrival," I texted.

"Please be quick, my friend is waiting along with me," he stated.

"Fine, I'll execute it swiftly. Bye," I ended.

I went to the bath and turned so agile and even Parnika returned the very next moment of my arrival. Now comes the greatest concern. What do I wear?! I pulled roughly twenty-five pairs out but ended stating that I have no clothes to carry! Though I do have a closet full of clothes, I still complain about the same as every girl does. At last, I inserted my hand deep into the trolley and got hold of a pair and put that on. It was pink and black combination top with a black legging and a black dupatta making the perfect union. I braided my hair to my left side, with no foundation nor talcum powder on my face like I did every day. I had a baby pink lip gloss to my lips and a little liner to my eyes. I got ready, even Parnika too. I held my handkerchief and mobile, putting on my sandals, directed towards the expo.

"Just rose, I'll be there in five minutes," I passed on a text.

"Yeah, waiting."

By the time I reached, he sat in the shade of a mango tree on the table in a black or almost gray-colored checks shirt and black denim. I went behind him, thought of calling CANDY, but it was Karthik and batch who were exactly opposite to us. I didn't utter a single word and diverted myself to the expo. I didn't tell Karthik about Ram, if I did, he would mock me. I went into the expo, started attending the projects. I twisted back to see if he was there, but I couldn't locate him outward.

"I am near the second windowpane observing you," he texted seeing me seeking for him.

I held my head and beamed. After a due course, I over checked but I couldn't find him.

"Where are you?" I asked.

"You are near the Mechanical project, right?" he said.

I turned back immediately. His entire attention was upon me, yet I was trying to escape his gaze.

I spotted him near the door. Yeah, he entered the room. I started smiling. He stood near the door contemplating at me. I was leaning back now and then, confirming if he was following or not. That was seriously a sort of happiness. I was trying to control my blush but it was getting portrayed by the sparkle in my eyes but don't know how far he could sense it. He almost succeeded wherever I go, I felt like being loved as I was treated special. We spent a lot of time there.

"I am leaving, Crush. I am pooped," he said.

I felt like stopping him, but that isn't a very generous act, my heart said. I said okay and lingered there a bit more and toured Renuka's project. After 10 minutes, I received a text from him,

"I went almost midway, but desired to see you and came back," he texted.

As soon as I read this, my face radiated as if a 1000 watts bulb. I tended back and he was there, I saw him. I was relishing this, all alone. Being watched is a very cute feeling and everyone loves it. The way he watches, and the way I respond marking him over, everything got a special practice that I ever made in my life. I wished to stay there for a bit more time but, it was Gowtham who came to see me and Ram who diverted him telling some sort of things. I didn't want him to grapple much and left. As I went, even he vacated.

I had lunch, then proceeded to my room. I am fatigued and fell on the bed as if dead.

Day 1 concluded with a lot of unusual endurance.

TECRUSH DAY 2

"You don't feel like the way I do, so, you don't comprehend my agony," he said that night.

"Is that? Fine, let me be your Candy and you will be my Crush. Let us swap our characters. Isn't that impressive?" I asked.

"Seems you can't handle your behavior, fine, take a chance," he told.

"Let's inaugurate it from tomorrow," I stated.

"As you wish," he left me a choice.

I wished him good night and fell asleep.

The next day, it was all non-technical events and we indeed had flash mob and closing ceremony in the dusk. We both registered for an event SBI which abbreviated, Srikakulam Bureau of Investigation in common. It's just similar to interpret a crime scene that will be depicted in a room. He even got selected for the final level IPL auction that will be conducted on the second day of the fest. Everything commenced for the second day.

Since I didn't go early on the day before, I got ready to witness the decorations people made. Parnika and I set everything right and proceeded to the fest. I reached the place, in a sea-green kurta with a white cotton pant and white dupatta on me, as the day before, a little liner and baby pink lip gloss, and my hair braided to the left side and my fingers painted with black nail paint. The byway was so creatively enhanced with emojis hanging on the top, there was a logo perfectly outlined, cut signifying that **I LOVE T CRUSH** with the thermocol sheet, and a minion in the opening attracted people. An Enfield dupe was situated in one of the entrances, all the walk was beautified with the multicolored lanterns.

As I am Candy and he is Crush, I started the conversation,

"Hey Crush, where are you?"

"I am in lambda cluster and where are you?"

"Please stay there, I am coming," I said.

"Hahaha, for?" he repeated my question.

"Just to watch you maa!" I answered his dialogue.

"Okay okay."

I, along with Parnika, moved to the lambda cluster and I was exploring for him.

"Where are you? I couldn't find you," I said.

"I saw you," he stated with pleasure.

"Where are you?" I asked him again.

"I am near the window," he added.

"I couldn't find you, Crush," I informed after checking for his presence.

"You can't see me, just a minute, let me come out," he said.

Then I saw him, he was in a white and red checked shirt and light blue denim. As I noticed him, the inconsistency in my optics made me get into the room nearby. I can't even reveal the way I felt. He crossed by the room glancing at me, I couldn't steadily concentrate his eyes! This might be the magic spell in the character. As he went, I stepped out of the room, and was following from behind. I was thoroughly occupied in the character and performing the finest. Later, he followed me to an extent leaving behind the truth about the character exchange. I spent some time in the cluster and he came after me with his friends, fortunately, they don't know about the way he feels for me. I had lunch and went to the room and he too does the same. Both of us avoid being in packed places and we were even depleted. To replete ourselves, we needed a power nap.

Before I leave, I urged him to come to the Mue cluster since I am Candy. His IPL auction was scheduled at the noon and once this is finished, we had our SBI. So we decided to attend the SBI at once.

Meanwhile, he arrived at the cluster. We heeded each other and left the place. We didn't let people know about any of our issues. I had a powerful sound sleep and woke up at 2:00 noon where SBI was programmed at 2:30, we got ready and rushed to the cluster and there took place an unexpected amendment in the schedule and IPL auction preceded the SBI, so he was already in the cluster and attended the auction.

"Where is the auction going on?" I asked.

"In omega cluster, class number three," he answered.

"Can I get in? Any girls over there?" I questioned him.

"Yeah you can, but there is no girl over here," he said.

"I'll bring some other girls, what say?" I asked him.

"Yeah, fine come," he told me.

I gathered some female cricket lovers and headed that room, in the due course, we started from our place, it was a drizzle that initiated. We all sped near room number three. I was attempting to open the door but couldn't, out of fear.

"I am in the corridor," I texted.

"I viewed you from the window," he replied.

"I am frightened to open the door," I said.

"Fine, anyways you better leave, there is no girl over here," he added.

"Okay, I'm flying, gonna attend SBI?"

"Hope it is at 2:30 right?, I may not attend," he said.

"Yeah, you will be still in the auction. Okay then, I'm gonna attend and let you know what's there."

"Okay, all the best," he wished.

I headed towards the competition. It got delayed due to rain and is going to start at 3:00 p.m. The volunteers stated. We three, Parnika, Nila, and I were wandering here and there. We were caught in the rain and soaked. Then was his text.

"Hey, it is raining, don't come out and play like a kid. Stay in, I'm reminding you again," he said.

"Ha, okay!" I told him showing my displeasure.

We ran into a classroom and sat speaking all the girly stuff. It was someone on the mike announcing about the event SBI which is going to start in few minutes and requesting all the participants to gather the venue. After listening, we went to the Alpha cluster, the venue.

Many people were standing out of a room like us. Because we hated waiting, we were the first to enter the room and participate. We were given five minutes and asked to observe the room without touching anything nor disturbing any of the articles over there. We will be given some questions to answer by the end, the event planners said.

We three went in, there was a laptop open but secured with a passcode. The door was imprinted with some handprints in red color, then, there were unusual shredded papers randomly projected in the room. A book, pen, coffee mug were on the table, and a dictionary was placed openly in one of the corners. There was a bed, a blanket on it, and a rope suspending to a fan, down a chair! A cloth was completely dipped in red paint, creating an illusion of blood, and was in one of the edges. Some quotes were affixed on the wall educating about law and rules. Few books related to the judiciary were on the desk. And were makeup kit, talc cum powder, comb, kajal, lip balm ordered on the dressing table in a row.

After examining all these, we were asked to answer three questions, one is to describe the crime plot, the second one is to justify whether it is a murder or suicide and the last one is to discover the culprit. We then took a paper and a pen and made a move to one of the classes with no people. We began analyzing the scene and I was texting him explaining the situation in SBI. We tend to think in all the ways possible and trying to put everything on paper.

"The flash mob is going to spring in few moments, I request all the students to go and witness the spectacular performance in prefab cluster," said the host on the mike.

Hearkening to this announcement, we were like fully replenished mobiles. Leaving everything behind, we answered that SBI with some senseless stuff and hastened near the prefab, but the IPL auction was still on. So, he didn't arrive. We reached, dancers both boys and girls were in blacktop and faded blue pair of jeans with white shoes. Girls with a ponytail, boys had their spikes and they stood in some sort of order. It took around fifteen minutes to start after our arrival. The very first song was boom! people were yelling out of exhilaration. The mob was getting to a level and we were literally out of bounds.

Then, entered Gowtham, he was exactly behind me, I didn't notice him but Nila alerted me. As I saw, I texted Ram that he was following me and asked what am I supposed to do. Can I warn him or get out of that place? He asked me to leave that area and I did the same. Gowtham tracked me throughout the way. I didn't know what to do and directed towards the girls' hostel where he had no access to come that way. I went to the room along with Parnika and Nila. We were worn out and we have a closing ceremony at 6 p.m. So, until then, we took a nap.

It was Virat bowling and me on the other side with a bat. I was about to hit a boundary, my dream was interrupted by Renuka's call. I didn't respond for the first two calls as I am out of consciousness. The third call was like hitting with Thor's hammer on my head. I woke up and answered, Renuka was asking me to come to the program and was nudging me by alarming that it was almost 6:30 p.m. Overhearing that, I woke up Parnika and we got ready in ten minutes and started towards the program. On my way,

"Where are you, Crush," I asked maintaining the same tempo from the morning.

"In the program and you?" he answered posing me a question.

"I am on my way."

We reached the place and assembled in the closing of the hall as it got filled. We were texting on WhatsApp and no way watching the program like we always did.

"Where are you sitting?" he asked.

"Just a row ahead of the faculty chairs," I answered.

"And where are you ?"

"Even, I settled in the end."

"Is that? Let me check," I was searching.

"Did you find me?" he texted.

"No Crush!" I said.

"Wait, I'll just stand and you can then see me," he told.

"Okay," I texted back.

He stood and then I just gave my eyes. The program was to an end and we were asked to go to the mess and have supper. We started, he thought of following me while we were leaving but due to a tremendous crowd departing at once, he couldn't find me. Somehow entered the mess. I took my meal plate and went to wash it, I was waiting near the water point and just hoisted my head towards the boys' mess. And it was! Candy, he was staring me, for the first time he was gazing me though I was studying him. Surprising! he didn't even let his eye splash and was occupied giving pleasure though I caught him. I tried to gawk the way he does but I couldn't, I was turning my head, couldn't converge!

Maybe, for this reason, people say,

We can never stare at your loved ones when they are gazing at us.

Here, I replaced love with like.

Maybe, this is the reason why people say, we can never stare at our liked ones when they are gazing at us!

THE DISTANCING DEED

He has been requesting me for my pictures a long back. In a due course, I could mount trust towards him, so, I granted him a few. Days were active, running like a jet plane. It is July when we started our conversation, and it is the first week of September now. We were almost in the third month of our journey.

I always dreamt of having a career in writing. Writing can either be poetry, stories, quotations, whatever but if it is literature, I would relish and get out of all my stress. That fine afternoon, I am in my class, a girl from the Mechanical department requested my class teacher for taking me out. She was one of my friends and I don't know why she called me out! I went and she was narrating me that, they inaugurated an organization, it's main intention is to obtain the college news and publish it in a college magazine named VEDHIKA.

So, the organization profoundly necessitated flexible content writers on the spot and further screening tests will be done later to make them permanent. The head of the team needed the sample of the magazine to be approved by the chancellor. The condition became an emergency as chancellor will be available in the college till that dusk. Another partner of mine from the Civil department was summoned to write an article. We were assigned a deadline and it's just an hour. So, we both were rather quick and presented it in time. The incharge appreciated our work and time sense. I am captivated that I made someone convincing with the work I love and that I'm engrossed in.

As I said, it was the first week of September and his birthday was on.

September 3rd was his day. I was checking for some gifts online. I couldn't pick what to present him and was scrolling the feed for something better. I was planning to offer him a pack of unique flavored KitKat chocolates but then I learned him stating that he will not be able to wear a new pair of costumes for this birthday as he misremembered them at home. We were left out with a week to travel home and his parents reporting from a long distance would severely sink them. And, boys were not allowed for an outing once we were given our mid terminal agenda.

Harking to this, I chose to present him with a t-shirt. I was exploring and then struck at a fabulous collection. I analyzed to sort the best out of them. Finally, it was a Martin Garrix black t-shirt with a few colored prints of the Marshmello logo on it. I preferred it. I placed an order and it would take a week for the order to deliver, the pop-out on my mobile said. If I present it directly to his hands, it would be feckless as I envied to surprise him. Then, I gave food for thought to my brain on how to astonish him. It was my schoolmate's brother who was studying in the same campus but a separate batch. Candy also stays in the same dormitory as the junior does. As I have some time for the order to reach me, I relaxed and went back to some other work.

After three days of the scenario, we were texting,

"Hey Crush, what are you doing?" he asked.

"I just came from the class, waiting for water to come so that I would rinse clothes," I replied.

"Okay, had something?" he questioned.

"Yeah, biscuits and chips. What about you?" I answered and asked him in return.

Meanwhile, I was distracted by a phone call from the VEDHIKA organization. They were inviting me to the Kappa cluster to attend the screening test for content writing. As I aspired to bury a pole of my interest in the college, I got a chance and didn't want it to slip off. I set everything right, I took my bag and was about to erupt. YOU KNOW YOU LOVE ME, I KNOW YOU CARE. JUST SHOUT WHENEVER, AND I'LL BE THERE, Justin's BABY it was, my phone started ringing. This time, another anonymous number.

I lifted the call, he was truly polite,

"Mam I'm from the online store. Hope I'm addressing to MIDHUNA on the other side."

"Yeah," I confirmed him.

"The order you placed has just arrived, will you be available at the bank to collect it?" he asked.

"I'll be there in ten minutes," and ended the call.

All I have to do is, collect the t-shirt getting down the three floors, then, place it back in my room surmounting the same three floors, later, walk a long distance to attend the screening test, return my room and then rinse my clothes! I was blown out by the wind!

I took Parnika accompanying with me to collect it, we went and received paying it from those that I have spared for my shopping. As I collected, we went to a nearby dormitory.

I unpacked it in a dilemma that it would fit him or not! The cloth and the design were impeccable and worth every penny. All that mattered was that size. I ordered for a medium size and hope that wouldn't even perfectly suit him because of his so-called skinny personality. I spent more than thirty minutes there, conversing some fruitless talk. By the time I began, my screening test was all ended. I missed it! What shall I do, if my luck doesn't gratify me? I worried a little but moved on. I packed it with some sticky paper notes set in it.

The first one, **No bday can be celebrated without a new dress. Please put it on if it suits you.** The second one, **If the medium size doesn't set you, it implies, you have to eat so hard that your flesh fits your shirt.** Third note, **Happy birthday CANDY!** Packing is done, how does it reach him? I thought of handing this over to my junior the day before his birthday and waited. Between the scene, I said to him earlier that I'm going to attend the screening test,

"How did you perform?" he asked.

"No, I didn't go!" I replied.

"Is everything fine?" he inquired.

"Yeah, all good. No worries."

"Then, why didn't you go? What's wrong?" he questioned.

"I had to rinse my clothes, so I didn't," I fibbed.

"There must be something inaccurate, I don't believe you. Tell me why didn't you attend?" he was interrogating.

"Nothing wrong, I'm telling you, right? I am fine," I peacefully texted.

"Writing is all your passion and I'm sure that you wouldn't let go off so easily, Promise?" he triggered.

"Don't ask me anything more, I went out on your purpose," I shortened.

"On my purpose? What is that?" he went chaos.

"I said you not to ask anything, Candy," I ended.

He was quite and we were back to our chat as usual after a fraction.

"How did your class go on?" I asked.

"It is English class I had, a nightmare to me."

"Why is that so!?" I questioned.

"My English lecturer ordered us to prepare for a presentation and every member of the class had to speak for at least five minutes."

"So, this is your nightmare?" I questioned.

"Yeah, I do have stage fright and cannot speak in front of everyone. I would bunk when my turn comes," he said.

"I have an idea to eradicate. You must try it," I texted.

"What?" he asked in chaos.

"From tomorrow, I'll be giving the topic and you have to present an article and submit me by 6 p.m every day," I challenged.

"!!!!" was his reply.

"Will you? or won't you?" I inquired.

"I can't just do it, Crush," he said.

"Fine, you can select your topic. This is an excuse that I can offer," I gave an option.

"Writing on my own topic? This is too tough! I can't decide the topic," he stated.

"Okay, fine. Write about the best moment of your life to date, this is your topic for tomorrow," I said.

"I don't have any best moments, Crush," he switched.

"Fine, write about the worst moment of your life," I gave an alternative.

"I ! don't have the worst moment too, Crush," he mumbled.

"Don't set me mad. Fine, I'm not going to talk to you till you send me the PDF of your article," I shortened.

"Why do you take such idiotic decisions? I don't understand!" he said.

I didn't reply to any of his messages from then.

I said, "We are not going to chat for ten days if there is no modification in your decision."

He pleaded, "Please don't give me such tasks. Ask me for some other thing, I'll definitely do it for you."

"Don't just plead me for any excuses. If you want me to speak, better write and send it. Candy, it is not for my sake. It's all for you, why don't you understand?" I argued.

"Why don't you understand me, Crush!" he said.

I was badly off with his responses, I didn't reply and came out of the chat.

I sternly decided not to speak to him for ten days.

It was around 9 p.m that day,

He asked me, "To which mail am I supposed to send the PDF?"

As I'm severely off, I didn't respond to his messages. After an hour,

He texted, "Fine, don't reply for any of my messages these ten days. I'll keep on texting."

I didn't even reply to that text.

I left it seen.

OUR FIRST CALL

It was approximately a week we stopped texting each other. I intended to address straight on his birthday, no before. No holiday would occur so agile as an exam does! Mid terminal three was on and as every engineering student practiced this, reading a day before the examination, so-called one-night batting where we burn the midnight oil, I even followed the same. If I score 10+ out of 15 marks studying for a single night, I could have challenged my class topper if I learned regularly, I wonder every student would assume this once the time passed. Those two days of the mid terminal, we covet rest as if we hadn't slept for a year and burnt the candle at both ends to gain better results.

Some of our deeds in our preparation be like, I would solemnly study till 1:30 a.m though my sleep thumps my eyelids. Once the clock hits 2:00 a.m, I just take a doze asking my friend to wake me up at 2:10 a.m. In between, I set an alarm for every two minutes once time crosses 2:05 a.m, and this was obviously, the trust I have with sleep.

September 2, the first day of the mid went on with absolute preparation and I perfectly scripted both the subjects. The second day doesn't matter me much as I am up to date with the syllabus, moreover, they were quite interesting, so are clear for me. After giving my exam, I straightly came back to the room and had a sound snooze like I ever did.

I had to hand over the gift pack to my junior at any cost. So, I called him after a comfortable rest and requested him to appear for collecting the wrapped box. He politely said he would. That night, I got ready to mess along with Parnika, held my bag with the present in. I almost reached the place where I urged him to come. I found him waiting along with his friend. I handed and said to preserve it safe and I would intimate the rest of the things on the phone. He nodded his head and walked towards his room and we moved to approach the mess.

I couldn't consume much, as I sensed my tummy full. I returned to the room, switched into nightwear. I opened books and started my preparation, I couldn't concentrate much. My thoughts were deceiving and I'm getting deviated. I expected this would happen, so, I already got everything planned a day before. I am okay with that pre-idea of the topics, but I wanted to have a recap. Somehow, I finished recapitulation by 11:00 p.m. I closed my books and packed in.

How shall I wish him? Can I call or text? Text is all we do throughout the day, that would be quite common. What if I call? Will that be okay? I don't generally call people on my own, why should I call him? It's his birthday, wishing him on call doesn't grant me sin. But will he consider it strange if I call?

Why would he! He likes me right, he wouldn't. But calling my opposite gender that too at midnight?! Birthday calls are late-night calls and some people would love to wish at 12 and it has been a trend, that doesn't matter at all. These were a loop of insecure questions that outnumbered one after the other. Finally, I firmed to call him. But I once said I wouldn't speak to him for 10 days? Since it was my prerogative, let me break the promise.

What shall I address him? Is it Ram or Candy !? What if, I address Ram! My God, it's damn ridiculous and completely unnatural to call him so. Let me continue with Candy. Will that make sense? Why wouldn't that make sense when I am habituated to call him and he was more habituated to respond to me so. That's all right and it's fine.

It was 11:45 p.m, my poor heart accelerated and I was out of control. I came out of my position, walking here and there, was into my imaginary calculations, smiling in between, frequently checking my mobile. This synopsis was interrupted by the thought, what if he doesn't answer my call out of fear?! Yeah, he is a bit frightened of me right! What shall I do? Then my inner voice advised me to call with a different number. I picked Parnika's number as a choice and held her phone and was earnestly waiting. I still wonder why my heart is pounding so restless! If a usual human heart, beats one hundred times per minute, then my heart was like, beating twice that of a common heart!

The clock struck 11:58 p.m, I saved his contact in Parnika's mobile as Candy. I opened the contact and got ready to call, it was 11:59:50 seconds. I made a call, the phone was ringing as my heartbeat got raised like a wave in the ocean. When he didn't answer, it fell off like the same tide. He answered the call.

"Hello!" I initiated.

"Hello," was his reply. I couldn't tally my imaginary voice with his'. It was different, a bit husky.

"Ram?"

"Yeah," he answered. Once he confirmed, it was exactly midnight.

"Happy birthday Candy!" I wished him. He was almost into astonishment. But then I said, "Don't panic please."

They were a few seconds lapse which created a silence between us. An excited, shy, matured feeling we have undergone. Who would talk first? Anyways silence is performing its finest job. Maybe it was my brain that turned off and my heart conversing with his'.

Then came the reply, "Thank you."

Parnika then asked me to wish on behalf of her, followed by Renuka.

"Hey, your sister and Renuka wished you," I intimated.

"Convey my thanks to them," he responded.

"I wonder if it is you that is speaking to me, your voice doesn't seem me so!" I doubted.

"It's me," he said with a bit uneasiness of the first talk over the phone.

"If it is you, then say my favorite hero?" I interrogated.

"Surya, Surya is your favorite hero," he stated.

"My favorite colors?" I posed.

"Black and white are your favorite colors," he answered with no doubt.

"Hey then, it is you, Candy," I said excitedly.

"Yeah, but someone said that they wouldn't speak to me for ten days!" he sarcastically sounded.

"By the way mister, I am not speaking to you but to Candy, my friend," I smiled.

He was about to respond, I heard some distinctive tones wishing him and a few were singing birthday song too, that was hilarious. So, then I halted the conversation and asked him to give his friends some time to spend on his occasion and before I end it, I asked him to call me back once they are done with the celebrations, as I have an important matter to tell him. He said okay and hanged the call. I was like holding a million-dollar smile on my face after our first call. I took one of my OOPS books and was reading with a scintilla on my face.

Parnika came near me and asked, "What are you reading?"

I said, "OOPS," showing her the book upside down in oblivion.

She corrected me turning the book upright and patting me on my back, but then she asked, "What subjects do you attempt for tomorrow's exam?"

"DBMS, OS, IR," I said with my tongue between teeth.

Then she said with jocularity, "Oh fine, just because it's his birthday, you are not going to take down yesterday's exam today."

I held my head for my innocent mispractice.

Seeing me so, she said, "Darling, I forgot to tell you something."

"What!?" I asked.

"Happy birthday!" she said turning her smile into laughter.

I, listening to that, rushed from my place to chase her. But then was a reply from him on WhatsApp that paused me. I turned back heading my room.

She shouted, "Midhuna, got your message?"

I pleased her not to shout by joining my hands. She giggled and even I did.

He then replied for my previous text.

I then asked, "Are you done with the celebrations?"

"Yeah, done."

"Shall I call you now?"

"Sure sure," he answered.

"Don't get frightened, I'll call you from my number this time," I insisted on him.

"Haha, okay," he said.

"Hello Candy," I initiated.

"Hello," he said.

"Where are you?" I asked.

"In the balcony," he answered.

"So, now you have a responsibility to finish. Go to the ground floor," I ordered.

"Ground floor?!" he exclaimed.

"Yeah, ground floor," I repeated.

"But why?" he asked out of confusion.

"I'll let you know once you reached," I said.

"Reached?" I questioned.

"On my way," he answered.

I could detect his agility in his footsteps.

"Go slow, you are anyhow weak. You will indeed get skinny," I said smiling.

"I reached, hello miss, I am not bony like you," he said.

"Fine fine, Go to room number 58," I directed him the way.

"58.....! Okay, going but where are you steering me?" he said.

"I'm sure that I am not directing to a burial ground nor a bhoth bungalow," I admitted sarcastically.

Our conversation lulled for two long minutes on his way.

"*Reached, what shall I do now?" he questioned.*

"Knock the door and call Shiva out from that room and say him my name," I said to him the directions to follow.

I could hear him, he did as I said. I wished to hear my name from him, don't know what but it delivered me an exceptional feeling yet a glad one. MIDHUNA! That pronunciation felt like a jolt of electricity to me. Then, my junior, Shiva gave him a bag with the wrapped box that I handed him last night.

He was about to leave, I asked Candy to thank Shiva. He said thanks and left.

"Open it in a place where you can find the least number of people and return the bag to him," I stated.

"Okay," he replied.

We spoke till 1:00 a.m. I, being a raconteur, unfolded many stories and had some sort of time-consuming talk.

I ended the call though I didn't want it to because speaking to him was like having frozen butterscotch in the sunny noon. I was treated special and felt like a cute puppy. But speaking to a guy late night isn't that advisable, so, I hang it up. After two minutes that I ended the call, I called him again.

"Hey, I forgot to ask you something, what will you say if your friends question about the present?" I asked.

"What shall I answer them?" he asked me to give him an idea.

"Reason is up to you but don't get my name in between, if you get it, people will surely cook rumors between us," I said with foresight about the future.

"Okay. I'll keep it out of their reach," he said.

"So!" I dragged.

"What will you do now?" he asked.

"Nothing much interesting, just a casual talk and then sleep," I answered.

"Oh! Okay."

"Fine, good night and bye," I ended.

Even he hanged up.

I felt like even he wished to continue the call. I had a text from him after ten minutes.

"Thank you, I liked the T-shirt and the scripts you wrote on it are lovable," he texted.

I replied with a smiley.

So, the first call ended with new knowledge of each other where my excitement turned into delight. Nothing much I knew about, but his voice! His birthday didn't end but started. Hoping for a better morning, I hit the hay.

APART FOR THE FIRST TIME

That morn, I felt crisp and clean, had a shower, besides I washed my hair, wore an ironed uniform, fish braided my hair, finally prayed God as if, it was my birthday. I then grabbed my bag, directed to the exam hall with full-fledged preparation for my mid. I got the exam paper, all I could retrieve was the conversation that I had the previous night. I wonder if it is only me feeling so, I wish him to hold the same as I do. How would I handle all alone? It would be better if feelings are distributed.

Did I fall for him?! No way possible, I just liked his company, my inner voice concluded the battle that I had with my brain. I finished my exam with deviations nevertheless gave complete satisfaction, with my presentation. I came out of the exam hall, took my mobile. I called Parnika to acknowledge her status. She didn't answer my call. So, it's much clear that she was still in the examination center. I have to wait a bit more time. I was checking for the notifications. I found his text on the tip,

"Hai, Crush"

I texted him, "Hey, how did you perform?"

"Third mid, right? I have to write well or else I will not have internals for the semester. So your question is HOW? I wrote well," he explained.

"Okay fine," I replied laughing at his explanation.

"Where are you?" he asked.

"Waiting for Parnika in Kappa cluster," I replied.

"Balance your bag to both the shoulders, so you will not be discomforted and move two steps backward, the sun wouldn't attack you," he said.

"Hey idiot, where are you to telecast all my actions?" I asked out of curiosity.

"Somewhere around you," he answered.

"Don't act smart Candy, tell me where you are?" I was searching for his presence.

"Don't worry much in searching me, I am to your right," he texted.

As he said, I instantly turned my head. I saw him, my almond rounded eyes got thinner as I smiled, my tiny lips went wide deepening the space on my cheeks into dimples, the very next while, he shifted his look. Someone said, people who likes you cannot give eye contact, he proved it correct.

"How long will you linger there?" he asked.

"I have to move towards lambda cluster and wait for your sister," I replied.

"Okay then, you go first and I'll follow you," he said.

I smiled a lot but didn't grant it out. Felt secure, seemed like a princess and he, being possessive lifted me high. I stepped towards Parnika's class, he followed me back. I frequently turned back smiling, checking if he was coming or not. That hoisted me with joy. Every time I turned back, I find him gazing at me. By the time I watch his eyes, he would straight away show his cheek. I reached, peeped into Parnika's exam hall. She was still scribbling. I waited outside the classroom for a while. He was around and I found him watching me but didn't expose myself completely to him. If someone finds us, they would issue this as a forward message. He then texted.

"Hey, with no delay, go somewhere. Don't stay in this cluster."

"But why Candy, what's wrong?" I asked out of interest.

"Crush, Gowtham is exactly opposite to me and if he finds you here, he would surely follow and irritate you," he concerned.

As I read the text, I vacated the place with no reply to him. I was walking fast in a hurry turning back for Gowtham's presence. I just faced the turning point, it was Candy ahead. I could feel his breath, too close we were and I was smiling at him, he struck over there for a moment and then accelerated. I didn't perceive if my smile would suspend people like this.

I moved to the Omega cluster. There were very few people, a peaceful area it was. I could then freely respire. I was enjoying nature and then, two guys rushed into the cluster abruptly. I was checking who it was, it is Karthik along with Candy. He, watching me, raced in and Karthik stood at the point where I am, to greet me. We were speaking to each other. Our talk was interrupted by a call, it was Parnika calling me. I answered her.

I said, "I am in Omega and it's better if you come here."

"What's better, puppy? Lambda is the shortcut to reach our dorms and Omega is so long distanced," she exclaimed.

"He is in omega. You come here, please," I pleaded in a cute voice.

"Oh, my poor lady! fine, stay there just watching, don't chew my brother. I'll be there in 5 minutes," she warned sarcastically.

"Take your own time," I said.

As I hanged the call, Karthik called Ram to join us. Karthik is the earliest one to know that Ram is crushing on me. He offered a chance to his friend to talk to his crush, so is me. Karthik doesn't have a minimum knowledge that we speak to each other and chat overnight.

He then said, "It's Ram's birthday today."

"Is it?!" I pretended.

But let him win, or else we both have to lose for him. He repeatedly called Ram to join but he didn't. He missed an opportunity. Then came Parnika, I started from that cluster along with her. At the extreme moment, I turned back as I wouldn't see him for the next ten days because of the Dasara vacation and I found him watching me. I smiled at him and left.

I changed my dress, packed everything, and got ready to leave. It was Parnika's father coming to take us home. Uncle arrived and we got our outpass to fly. I called Candy to say him that I'm starting. He didn't answer the first try, and he got connected with the second attempt.

"Candy, I'm leaving."

"Now?"

"Yeah now, bye," I concluded.

"Bye, take care," he replied.

I disconnected the call and he texted me that Karthik is next to him so he couldn't speak properly.

I wanted to see him once before I leave but I am almost outside the gate. We boarded the auto.

"You had nothing in your stomach yet skipped lunch," he said.

"You don't know, I have a strong body and won't regularly fall sick."

"Yeah, very strong body! Even kids would consume more. Have something, Crush," he concerned.

"Yeah, we are heading to a nearby restaurant."

"Okay, fine," he replied.

"By the way, how will you go home, bus or train?" I questioned.

"We are still confused. It is your friend who has to decide and you are boarding train, right?" he responded.

"Yeah, boarding train. Is the final decision with Karthik?" I asked.

"Yeah!" he stated.

"Fine, take care. Leave me a text when you pick your source of travelling, happy journey," I concluded.

"Sure, you indeed take more care, travel safe," he said.

"Hahaha. Fine, I'll. Bye," I ended.

After twenty long minutes, was a text from him.

"Crush, we are in the railway station," he said elatedly.

"What! At the station? Are you boarding the 2:30 p.m train?" I asked.

"No Crush, seeing the crowd in the station, changed our opinion to board a bus. Gonna leave the platform soon," he told.

"Where are you? I wanted to see you one last time before I leave," he said in hope.

"Almost reached," I said.

"What colors did you put on?" he asked to identify me easily in the crowd.

"I am in a brown shirt on black denim," I hinted.

"Okay," he replied searching me in the crowd near auto that just arrived and it is the auto in which I'm.

I found him from a long distance along with a group of boys. Even Karthik was among that gathering. So, I couldn't raise my head. Uncle went to the next platform to get the boarding tickets. Parnika and I started towards the station. On our way, Karthik suspended us and was inquiring about our journey. Meanwhile, Ram was staring, though my eyes were towards Karthik, I could feel his looks from one of the corners. Our wish of seeing each other for the last time before leaving was indeed successful. Later, we went to the station. I wanted them to board the same train as we did but they were about to leave and made a way to the bus stop. He saw me till he could find me from the auto.

We somehow boarded the packed train with a lot of effort. After an hour, I received a call from Karthik.

"Hey Midhuna, there came a gang of fellows inquiring about you," he said.

"What?! About me!" I asked in chaos.

"Yeah, they are asking everyone in the station. They are from Saradha college. I could recognize their uniform," he said.

As I heard the college name, I got hold of the name, Anuj, who has been loving me from my schooling.

"Oh! But what did you say them?" I asked.

"I said I have no idea about you and informed my friends in the station to answer the same," he added.

"Thank god! You rescued me, Karthik. Thank you," I thanked him.

"Anything serious?" he asked.

"No no nothing, I'll tell you later," I said.

"Fine, take care," he concerned.

"Sure, thanks a lot," I ended the call.

As I ended the call, I received a text from Candy, the same story that Karthik said to me.

"My anger is out of bounds Crush, I am unable to tolerate this," he turned wild.

"Candy, I'll tell you later," I tried to calm him.

"Who the hell is that guy to ask about the girl I like!?" he was griming.

"Candy, please cool down. Have a safe journey. I'll clear everything once we reached home," I tried to chill him.

"What's wrong if you tell me now?" he interrogated.

"Candy, you are turning aggressive. We will discuss it later," I shortened.

"Fine, don't ever tell me anything," he stated and was offline.

He was out of my curb and was repeatedly urging me about that guy. He was ferocious at the moment, I'm afraid. What if I say he had been loving me since my schooling?! He would surely turn feral. So, I terminated the chat. He wouldn't understand that.

TURNING WILD

I reached my home town at 6:00 p.m after an arduous journey. My papa came to pick me. I saw him at the station, and couldn't restrain myself. I was getting down the stairs of the platform rapidly. My eyes glistened seeing him, I accelerated, held my luggage to both the shoulders, and started racing towards him. Why wouldn't a hosteler have such a reaction, missing their parents for five months? I understand I am going to stay with them for the coming ten days but the first sight would have an equal joy living the next days. I hugged my dad so tight that even air wouldn't find void between us. He took my baggage from me and I locked my dad's little finger with mine and strolled towards the entrance.

I was waiting while my dad went to get his bike. He stopped exactly in front and turned the accelerator up, I placed my hand on his right shoulder and hopped on the bike behind him. It takes around twenty-five to thirty minutes to stretch towards my home from the railway station. I continuously had a productive conversation in that half an hour with him. I commence it with the journey and conclude it with mischievous acts I do in the college. He always wonders how my friends are tolerating all the foolish childish acts that I do.

My papa would never neglect to ask me about Andy Alexander, Barbie, Cutie, and Denny. I would always say,

"Andy and Barbie are fine, but this Cutie is not at all listening to my words, Denny is not letting me concentrate on my lecture in the classroom."

He would forever pity those dolls and self regret purchasing me. We reached home in just twenty minutes, less than that of normal duration. The accelerator might have known that I arrived, so it would have automatically raised.

I rang the calling bell, it was my mom with a wide smile and Surya, my younger brother whom I could see, as the door opened. Surya took my bag off my shoulders and placed it on the chair and I was asked to get in and take shower so I would have something to eat. I went, had bath for half an hour having no hurry that someone would wait for my return to get in, no hurry of being late to the class, and no hurry for the food in the mess to turn over, felt like a shackles-free creature.

I came out, charged my mobile, stowed my luggage in my room, and sat down for dinner. I assembled in the corner chair of the four-chaired dining table waiting for my dad. We had dinner, sizzling chicken fried rice. That reddish-brown crispy chicken fingers, light yellow egg crumbs moistened my jaws. Curd raitha was complementing. I forgot about my phone, his chat, and more importantly, his anger, savoring the food.

I said all the stories of college to my mom and brother and the repeat telecast of those that I told my dad on the journey. We hit the hay too late compared to all the regular days at home. I stirred up at 11:30 dawn. I switched my mobile data on with that drowsy eyes. As I turned on, I was flooded with a lot of messages. They were almost 300 messages from 7 contacts. Among those 300, 100 texts from few contacts and random groups and those 200 alerts were from a single contact. That was from him. Those messages read,

Hey.

I reached!

Just now.

Tell me what's wrong with that idiot?

You said you will narrate everything once we reached home.

Didn't you reach yet?

Fine, text me after reaching.

Meanwhile, I'll fresh up and come.

Didn't still turn up?

I'll even have dinner and come very soon, if you arrive online in this sort of time, please wait for me.

I'll be back in ten minutes.

What's wrong?

After two hours…

You will surely reach by this time.

But, you didn't still text!

Is everything fine?

Reached safely?

I'm turning mad at you, don't let me. Reply fast.

A continuous flow of 50 angry emojis in order hit my screen.

He once said, he doesn't like to give an angry emoji to me, but today, he does.

Okay then, zip your secrets in your own pockets, don't give a chance to any pickpocketer.

Tell me directly, if you don't want your secrets to be revealed, I'll not trouble you again.

Good night

I'm sleeping

Bye

And the same flow of angry emojis continued for more 100 times.

I expected that it would become a dreaded conversation seeing those texts. I replied to him in the morning, but he was not giving his senses to my talk. I wished to flee from the circumstance. Then, I narrated the whole story of that guy, even then, he was mad at me. I tried to convince him yet my trails went in vain. I came off the chat rebuking the marquee on my forehead. I didn't think this would set fire. I brushed and had a shower, skipped my breakfast, it was almost my lunchtime. I sat down for lunch and hunting for my favorites on the dining table. As I gulped, I closed my eyes enjoying the taste of the food that I missed. I ate till the void in my esophagus overflowed.

I was walking here and there just to empty my stomach holding my mobile. He then texted, came up with a strange topic near me. He was revealing about one of his neighbors named Chaithra, who was a year younger to us. She was a type of girl who would wait for his arrival and glue her eyes on him. And she was that daring one, who waves a hand as he passes by. I was set on the flame. If I was over there, I would have killed that idiotic lady.

"How come you knew that she is watching you?" I asked concealing my anger.

"I just saw her gazing me," he replied.

"So, you even saw her. Fine, let this whole world burn, but I am not going to speak to you," I vexed.

"Listen, I saw her casually," he said.

"How dare you speak about a girl, that too near me?!" I fumed.

"I said you this, just like all other things that I share," he stated.

"Fine, don't speak to me. I'm tired of listening to all your stories. I can't stand it," I inflamed.

"Okay, don't turn aggressive. Let me speak, can I?"

"Don't try to convince me, I'm mad at you," I enraged.

"Listen, you are the only girl I give my eyes with all my senses live," he stated.

"But you even saw her, go with your girl. Chat with her, leave me alone," I burst out.

"Crush, the same way I felt when that guy came to ask about my girl, how dare he inquire about you near me. Just think how I feel, try being me," he explained.

I replied with a wide smiling emoji. So serious battle ended with a peaceful smile.

"You know what Crush, I like you so much," he said.

"Is that?" I asked laughing.

"You won't understand until you are in my place," he told.

"Candy, I'm reminding you again. It's just Crush, a short term feeling that wouldn't last long," I added.

"Okay, leave it. You are loose, don't even have an idea of what you speak," he ended.

"Fine, I'm loose right?!" I added a grief emoji.

"You are loose, but I even like you," he compensated saying so.

"What are you up to?" I asked smiling.

"Watching the movie," he said.

"Oh fine, carry on," I told as I have nothing to speak.

"You know what Crush, here hero just mocks heroine LOOSE and she cries out very cutely as you do," he said.

"Hey, I even like that scene. I'm too watching the same movie," I joined.

Coincidence always seemed to be following us. We had approximately the same tastes and interests.

"Till today, it was one of my favorite movies but from today, this scene became my favorite that reminds me of you," he expressed.

"Even I love to watch it," I blushed in.

We had a casual talk and then, my mom called me. I said him that I have to leave and ended the chat with a bye. He again replied to me with the same that I texted. I again said bye, the incessant chat didn't come to an end, I then used an emoji which was a cute duckling. He replied that with another emoji of the same kind. I named my emoji as SWEETY and asked him to name his emoji, he was laughing for my words.

"What! Naming an emoji? It's totally funny. Go with your choice, name it as you like," he said.

"Um... TWINKLE?" I asked for his opinion.

"All right," he replied with a thumbs up.

And then, we ended naming our emojis. Continued practicing them to end our chat every time we needed.

EXPIRED CRUSH

It's time for me to vacate, my merriment frittered away time. I came home with untidy, messy, clothes. I am traveling back with tidy, ironed ones. I came home skinny, and dark, running back chubby and fair. The only difference is, I came home with a lot of anticipation and excitement but returning with boredom, no elation, moreover an ached heart that is unwilling to leave but has to! My dad dropped me to college.

The college gate was like the entry to perdition. I am back to those days where, I have to wait until the one in it, to step out to use the restroom. I worked up jotting the dates for a vacation, once it is over, I strike it off counting the left out days for me to rebound home. Waiting for the unsavory food in a queue to compliment our stomachs when the empty bellies reminded our mind about their existence. It has been four years that I lived in the hostel. Everything around has been usual and I was habituated to it.

I was unpacking all those my mom stuffed. I was then hit with a message on my phone screen.

"Crush?" he texted.

"Hey, you are no longer supposed to address me Crush. The three months period is all over and as per my

knowledge about an unknown writer, a crush and a toothbrush are to be changed within three months. I am your expired crush now," I said.

"You know what, you are not my crush. You are more than Crush and less than love," he stated.

"What is this, less than and more than? I feel like attending a mathematics lecture," I replied.

"Nothing complicated, google the accurate word which defines the feeling, more than crush and less than love," he insisted on me.

I googled and the result out was ATTRACTION.

"So, you got attracted to me?" I questioned.

"Yeah, you pulled me to your side. You are a magnet, and had the power of drawing people," he said.

"Stop flirting man!" I told raising my eyebrow.

"I am not flirting, I am truly attracted. You swept me off my feet," he elated.

"Seems like movie dialogue. Whatever from today, I am not your crush," I reminded.

"Okay, you are not my crush but you are my magnet," he said.

"Hey, mark this, you are beyond Crush and beneath love," he added.

Reading those lines, I was tingling with excitement.

I once said to him that I don't speak to those who loves me. Is that the reason for developing such peculiar notes! I churned my brain. Is he loving me? What if he loves? Do I have an answer? No! Then why do I think about all these questions? I cleared everything from my brain and enjoyed his company. My feelings for him were obscured.

That evening, I was busy braiding my Cutie. Parnika was completely immersed in drawing her charts. She, being a mechanical student had to undergo all that stuff. I asked if she needs my help, but she said that I cannot handle those minute measurements and mentioned that all the students of the Mechanical were to submit their charts in two days. If I start helping her, for sure she will be in due.

"Two days!?" I exclaimed. "Today is Saturday and you need to submit it by Monday? Poor fellows!" I pitied.

I was then hit with a thought of Ram,

"Are you done with the drawing charts?" I inquired.

"Nope, I'll complete them in the lab tomorrow," he answered.

I asked Parnika if she had planned to head to the drawing lab tomorrow.

She was about to ask me the same if I can accompany her to the lab. I conveyed my acceptance. I thought not to waste time, instead execute my DBMS queries taking my laptop.

"You know this, we are coming to the drawing lab tomorrow," I informed him.

"Is it? At what time?" he asked with excitement.

"Maybe at noon," I said.

But then he texted again, "Fine, I may not come at the same time as you go because if someone finds me near you, they would tease you for sure," he concerned.

After reading it, I felt like ordering him to come but he stated a reasonable circumstance and withdrew myself. But I'm quite sure that he would somehow come.

That noon, I got ready to mess and then we gonna head towards the drawing lab. I made myself comfy in a peach Kurti with a tiny white printed design all over, a white ankle fit cotton pant presented me in perfect attire. A little eyeliner, my hair braided to my left usual and baby pink lip gloss complimented. Parnika and I had lunch in the mess and made a move approaching the lab.

We reached, the room was unoccupied, all that I caught sight of were those tall chairs with no arms, spacious desks arranged in no order, and the deadly silence. The hall had two beams rising midst. I sat facing the window, opposite the main door. The window which was partially closed induced the cool breeze to company me. And Parnika sat two chairs apart comforting herself for the flexibility in the drawing. I initiated my work and she even began. An hour later, my mobile was banged with a notification. I felt like everything over there was advising me to put a cork in. So, I muted the volume and then looked over the alert that I received.

"Where are you?" read the text from Ram.

"In the drawing lab," I replied.

"I want to come as I took a fancy to you. But I wish, you should never face hostility because of me," he said.

I replied with a smiley and closed the chat.

I was then drifted to those sounds from a mass of boys who were making the way towards the ground. I stood by the window and listened without turning around. A cricket kit or more was being shared by the clump, one held bat, the other running with the ball, few with the wickets, some tying up their pads, a guy wearing the helmet, and posing to the camera. I was chuckling, witnessing their deeds. And then, I found Ram stretching his direction to the ground burying his head into the mobile screen. My mobile beeped.

"Are you still in the lab?" he asked.

"Yeah," I said.

"Look into the window," he said.

"Just a second," I texted.

I found him hunting for me and I giggled more but pretended that I didn't find him. As I said, he stopped for a while and was staring more extensively. I feasted my eye on him from the other window. He got going with the other window one by one. I kept me out of his sight locking up behind the wall. He was perplexed but I am relished watching him without his notice. His desire of finding me was entirely adorable.

"Fine, I'm leaving," I informed.

"Leaving! Fine, stay safe," he dejected.

CAN SOMEONE GUARANTEE FEELINGS?

"I've learned that people will forget what you said, people will forget what you did, but people will never forget how you made them feel." Maya Angelou

One such person whose deeds didn't fail me remember even with four years of our separation. He is named Pradeep, my closest brother who elevated me when I am feeble, I invariably found his shoulder when I am low. I laughed so uncanny, behaved extremely rough but he never complained instead lived in my moments. I would never pretermit the day when I was talking to him over the phone and didn't notice that my mobile was on its final legs and dead.

I charged it and slept that night. I switched it on in the dawn, I was aghast at the notification that read, **YOU HAVE 1337 MISSED CALLS FROM PRADEEP BRO.** I called him with no delay, I asked the reason for so many attempts to contact me, he said that, he was tensed with the sudden switch-off of my gadget. And tried to reach me the entire night and just took a nap. I was contented with his answer.

After so long time, I received a call from him. He came up with two fruitful news that, his first book got published and the review was too good. The second one was out of the box that he was offered a job in a well-reputed company that drove towards his interest. The happiest thing here was the HR of the company directly called him reviewing his book, she was amazed by his dedication and proposed a job amid his BTech. Then, within a month or two, he would be promoted. I was amused by his records.

We had a casual talk and then he, being the central pillar and close-knit to his HR, recommended me for a summer intern in his company. With his assurance, HR trusted with no issue. He was telling me all details about the intern which deals with content writing and marketing for three months. All that mattered was the locus, Bangalore! I didn't live apart from my parents, that too, it's far-off. I was set ready and all I needed is permission from my parents. I know I would get it if I endeavor. Struggling for dreamwork isn't that tough.

I ached to share this gleeful news to Candy, I felt like conveying it through a conversation.

"Hey, are you engaged or unoccupied?" I texted.

"Occupied for others, free for you all the time," he dramatically said.

"Stop kidding man, I have a piece of happy news to tell you," I told him.

"Yeah, unoccupied," he replied.

"Can I call you?"

"Sure Crush," he answered.

I called him,

In desperation to talk to him, I left myself behind.

"Hello Candy," I initiated.

"Hello, had dinner?" he asked.

"Yup and you?" I questioned back.

"Yeah had, what's the news. Is it propitious?" he asked sarcastically.

"Excitement to me, probably grief to you," I chuckled.

"If it is a delightful one to you, that will bring a smile in me too," he said.

"Say the same after listening to me," I said.

I narrated the whole story and I declared that I will not be available on the campus for two months as it is a three-month intern and we were given only a month as summer vacation. Silence occupied between us, everything around us was despair, air tangled and then,

"Ram!?" I broke the stillness.

"Fine, just two months, right? No matter how far you are, my heart still feels you close," he said in an unwretched tone.

I accepted tranquility to hold again, his words were poisoning me with love. He gradually built a cottage of LIKE in me but I didn't want that to happen. Don't know what made him break peace this time,

"Are you happy to leave?" he asked.

"Yeah, I am. Just to tell you this, I called. You better proceed with your work now. Good night," I said abruptly.

I could sense my digression and was not normal anymore. I ended the call, but his words were still whirling madly in my brain. I didn't want love to enter between us. I needed void to be maintained but then, I realized that we were being jammed. I witnessed many love stories that had misery in the end.

"Is everything fine, magnet?" he texted.

I took a big decision, in fact, a groundless one. I know that it would shake him off. I didn't expect that would stir a hornet's nest.

"Fine, it is Crush you had when you don't know me, right?" I asked.

"Yeah, now you are beyond crush," he elated.

I landed up saying, "The only difference from then and now is, we being contacted. What if this attraction grows more? I don't want anything to come in between, you have been my close friend all way now and wish this to be continued."

"What are you speaking about? I don't understand," he said.

"Promise me that your emotions would not stretch anymore," I asked.

"What!? Can someone guarantee feelings?" he said.

"If you cannot guarantee, then stop speaking to me," I shortened.

"What are you speaking Crush, I don't even have a clue about your talk," he said in chaos.

"I am perfectly all right and clear with my words," I stated.

"You better say that you wish not to speak to me anymore, why to cook up everything?" his forbearance questioned.

"I don't need to bake something, I am just telling this for our sake. I don't want our feelings to be unsacred," I tried to convince.

"All you need to do is a promise Ram, what's wrong with it?" I added.

"Ram! Fine, addressing is being changed with decisions. I wonder how this happened at an instant," he said losing his patience.

"Nothing like serious Ram, just an assurance," I said.

"I can never guarantee my feelings!" he stated boldly.

"Then, are you sure that your feelings for me will develop?" I asked.

"That's what I'm telling you. How can someone have a grip over their feelings?"

"I can never affirm that my feelings for you would either grow or collapse. If you are aware, just tell me how?!" he questioned.

I pretended to be on cloud nine but had no answer to his questions.

"Don't just ask me anything. All that I needed at the instant is your promise," I said.

"Fine, hope you are clear with your words. I'll better stop speaking rather promising my feelings to you," he was clear with his reply.

"Done," I said and ended our three-month conversation with a full stop.

I wanted him to speak, at the same time, I even required him to assure! I never expected my calculations would deteriorate. This pulled over our bond and went pear-shaped. I was screwed up yet didn't hang in there.

I blocked his contact on all the social media that I'm available having a lump in the throat. He then texted me on Truecaller! But even then, I just read the message and left without replying. This will hurt more than blocking. He texted for some days and slowly dropped messaging. But his indelible impression didn't fade.

We stopped articulating to each other that made me secretive again.

He didn't ignore me completely but had an eye. He watched me when I am in and out of study hour. He passed by my class for no cause but to see me. I faked ignoring him but I still don't know why I am doing so? I too noticed every deed of his' but pretended just to widen the breach, that too unwillingly.

It was so horrible being distanced almost for a month. I don't know what made me do so but felt suffocated. I thought I would give him the cold shoulder but all I did is, unblocked his contact on Whatsapp and implored him to speak to me after a long gap of thirty-one days. He said NO! This set me on fire and felt insulted for asking him. I lost my self-respect but then tried to preserve our bond. I wanted a genie to come out of the bottle. He knew everything about me and elated watching me but didn't wish to speak to me like before. Without my notice, the cottage that is being constructed in me even got painted well of LIKE.

I found no one to pour oil on troubled waters. How will I find someone to clear, when I did all the mess? I have struck my foot with an ax but my desire of making him speak as before is live just like pie in the sky.

THE U-TURN

I had a routine and stereotypical life. We got ready to mess that evening. I consumed too little and we headed back. I always preferred to have an ice-cream when I'm feeble. We three, Parnika, Nila and me went to the canteen to have one. I sat in the ground solely, Parnika went to get the ice-creams and Nila was attending a call. That night, when all the lamps were turned off, doors were shut, the whole atmosphere is free, clear sky overhead, stars twinkling bright and I was gazing at the moon thinking that he was doing the same. His thoughts were spattered on me, he was a drug and I am trying abstinence. I was then handed my chocolate flavored Cornetto cone. Parnika bought a vanilla flavor for her and Nila loved a Pistachios one. We sat together in a triangle. I slowly unwrapped and savored my first byte. Nila was again encountered with a call and she went out answering it.

I shared everything with Parnika, she then asked how childish am I to ask for guaranteeing feelings? She consoled me and promised that she would update his deeds. I was a bit relaxed, the reasons were both ice-cream and Parnika for my ease. We left that place disposing of the wrappers in the nearby dustbin. I was running and jumping on my way to the room. We reached, I took a refreshing shower and came back. I engaged with my books to complete my assignment. It was 9:45 p.m, I am almost in the midst of my task. Renuka opened my room door so abruptly and pulled me off my bed and took me to her favorite spot in the dormitory.

"Renu, what's wrong with you? Why did you bring me here so swiftly?" I questioned.

"I am not well," she answered.

"What happened?" I was asking, placing my arm over her forehead to check the temperature.

"Hope you are doing well with your health, you have no temperature too," I added.

"I have no issues with my state of being," she replied.

"Then?" I asked.

"I could feel the transformation in you, Midhu. You changed a lot. Don't know what's wrong but putting all your efforts in texting your Virat. You are not even wishing me good night," she expressed her grief.

"Virat?" I asked in chaos.

"Ram. I named him Virat as you both have him as your common interest," she explained.

"Oh, I got it, so this is your problem. Renu, he is different and you are too. You remained from the very beginning and he came amid," I said.

"That is the issue. Yes, 3 months probably you are in contact with him. It is far lesser time than the years which we have spent together. I hate it if someone is prioritizing you. I'm jealous!" she said.

I laughed out loud and stated, "Shall I tell you a piece of happy news?"

"What?" she asked raising her chin.

"We are not talking to each other. You will not have conflicts anymore. Okay?" I asked hugging her.

"Is it? What happened?"

"Nothing serious, just a small concern," I said and closed as she hated a conversation of his'.

"Hey Midhu, you can say me. I am not that heartless to laugh at your sorrow though it brings happiness in me," she asked pleasingly.

I was about to narrate and Parnika called my name loud from the room, I went responding to her taking Renuka along. I entered the room. I then remembered the assignment that I left, I rushed near the PC and my notebook. Renuka said she would attend to the story in my free time and left wishing me goodnight. I even wished her good night and came back to work. I finished my work and looked at Parnika. She was staring at me.

I was then struck,

"What's wrong maa, why are you staring at me?" I asked.

She raised her brows.

"Hey, you called me, right? But why?" I reacted to her cast.

"So, if I call you for the birth ceremony, it's like you respond to the funeral. Very responsible and quick enough too," she said sarcastically.

"I merged into work, I forgot! I am sorry. Tell me what's the matter?" I begged, clutching my ears.

She began to say,

"My friend Rohan called me yesterday. He said about my brother," she paused.

"Ram?" I asked for clarification.

"Yeah," she answered.

"What did he say?" I asked.

"Promise me that you would not ask Ram nor go dull," she mentioned.

"First tell me!" I was crossing my fingers for what that had gone wicked.

"Rohan went to his friend's room and my brother too joined. Then, Rohan's friend was saying Rohan about

Ram's proposal list. He even mentioned that though he got too much following, he is yet admiring Midhuna," she paused.

"Fine, what's inaccurate to worry?" I asked understanding the context very clear.

"Then my brother replied that he loves you!" she halted.

"No, he would never say so. Hope Rohan might have listened in a wrong context. I choose to dissent," I said clearing.

"I know, you would not concur but I even questioned Rohan thrice. He is bold enough with his words," she said.

Listening to that, I was almost aflame but then, was sulking over the moment. I was down for what he had done to date but this incident was the last straw. I ever asked him not to put our bond in public due to which people develop rumors. But this time, he didn't consider my words and left them aside as he left my memories!

It was like a backstab. I felt him the closest and shared every sort of my deeds. He even promised me that he would never expose our things. And today was like, he threw me, our memories and chats into a dump yard. I lost my faith in him. I was fickled, what else would I do for this!? I had no clue for his doings. With all that had happened, I was really at the end of my tether.

I unblocked his contact and told him off for his pointless acts,

"What are you thinking about me!? Can someone cheat like this? You made me a puppet and played as you wish. I still wonder if it is you, to whom I spoke for three months?" I texted in despair.

"What happened? What are you speaking about?" he asked.

"Acha, you don't know anything right?" I fumed.

"What did I do?" he replied.

"Didn't you say that you loved me to Rohan's friend?" I asked.

"What are you speaking? I didn't say anything like this," he confessed.

"Don't dare to lie near me Candy, sorry, Ram!" I responded correcting his name.

"I didn't say him like that," he told.

"Then, what did you say?" I asked frowning.

"I said I like you and truly crushing on you. That's it," he stated.

"I have proof, at least now, admit that you bluffed. I would be happy when you hurt me with the truth than comfort me with a lie," I asserted.

"How can I accept other's faults? Fine, you said you had a proof right? Please bring it out," he demanded.

Ifs and buts evolved between us. Our views were brought together and were badly debated.

I texted Rohan, but he was not online. It was 11:30 that night, so I said I'll send him in the morning and ended the chat in despondency. But then after 15 minutes, Rohan responded to my text and said the same as Parnika told me. I thought I would have a voice note recorded for better proof.

The next morning, I went hurry to class, so I couldn't make a call. I was free in the evening. I ringed Rohan, I asked him what's the matter and requested for a detailed explanation. He said everything.

"Ram said he liked you," he said.

I was surprised by his response.

"You texted that he loved me last night," the surprised me asked.

"I was a bit unclear with like and love," he answered so innocently.

He doesn't know his innocence has hurt a heart! I criticized Ram though he was telling me the truth. I never gave him a chancc to speak nor tried to believe.

I apologized him,

"I'm sorry, it was a misunderstanding. The fault is all mine, what happened is," he interrupted me.

"Fine, leave it. I know about you, don't ask me for an apology. I can understand you," he said.

"But, why don't you listen?" I asked.

"Do you have anything else to say?" he questioned me trying to end the conversation.

"No!" I said.

"Okay then, tell me if you face inconvenience with my deeds. Bye," he concluded.

"Bye," I ended.

I regretted rebuking him. No one would get to acknowledge my tears just because I am weeping in the rain. It is only me who can sense the pain yet no one bothers. I am at my wits' end trying to confess him. Though it was not my mistake, I had to endure the worse.

CONFESSION OR DENIAL

It was one afternoon, Sathwika and I were remaining near my classroom for the previous batch to finish their weekend so that we can enroll to attempt. I was sensing the essence of greenery all around, the little bird's chirps that made me reminisce my low-pitched talk in my infancy, the tall Teak tree that grew high, virtually touching the skies. I was engaged observing all those from the door and it was Ram approaching my way. He peeped into my class checking my presence.

I noticed him noticing me but acted as if I didn't notice him noticing me. He passed by my classroom. I felt, this was the appropriate time to dispatch my remorse as he was stretching single. I asked Sathwika to accompany me, we hiked back of him to an extent. She doesn't know where and for what we are going, but blindly followed me without questioning anything. Sathwika was commenting,

"Midhu, see that gaunt guy ahead. He would fly away with the wind," she laughed out pointing Ram.

"Maybe people like him are blessed yar, not everyone can fly free of charge," I cutely opposed smiling.

"He seems so innocent," she said.

"Looks can be deceiving lady. But people who resemble innocent may not possess innocence," I honestly opposed.

I progressed too close, but I couldn't muster the strength to speak to him. I diverted in the opposite direction to his'. I hope he marked us following him but didn't at least take a turn. I moved from there and headed towards the exam hall.

That night,

"You don't bother who I am, you never admired me too. How wicked you are to take my breath off? Made me a puppet and performed all your plan. I may forget but I'll never forgive you, you burnt me alive. I am incapable to ingest the truth, that you faked your feelings towards me. I'll kill you," I actuated with a weapon in my hand approaching him yelling out his name, RAM…!

Parnika nudged me splashing water on my face. I got up from that deadly nightmare. I was given some water to drink. She patted me on my shoulder, sat next to me, and asked what had happened. I said all that I had witnessed in the dream. I desperately ought to show my regret and needed him to accept. Trusting is the next task but I wished him to listen to all my words firstly.

It was 12:30 that night, I didn't fret anything at that moment. I called him with all the load in my heart. I wish to get it down admitting my mistake. He disconnected the call and addressed with a text message,

"What happened?" read the text.

"Answer my call," I texted back.

"For what?" he asked.

"First respond to my call, I'll tell you everything," I implored him to answer my call.

"What's wrong? Did you get hurt with any of my deeds or what?" he asked.

I was vexed and even worried with his reply. Concealing my anger and ego, I called him again and texted,

"Please answer," I begged beyond my limit.

"What's the matter?" he questioned.

"About us," I answered.

"Fine, I'll answer but speak nothing and just listen to your words," he finally agreed.

"Okay," I said. Even I exactly wanted this.

He answered my call. I expected him to own a moratorium on his anger.

"Hello, am I clear with my voice?" I asked.

"Yeah, tell me what you envied to convey?" he bluntly questioned.

I was attempting to bring the subject up and he broke me off saying,

"My mom said not to respond to any calls after 10 at night. Sorry, I can't stay on call for a too long time, quit beating around the bush, and finish it fast," he replied repartee.

How would someone undergo listening to this? I felt being ignored and battered too. I had it up to here. At one point of time, I was treated special, but now, it is ignorance. I never tasted it, the flavor today made me leave out the situation.

"I'm sorry to waste your time. I just forgot everything that I wanted to tell you, good night and goodbye," I disconnected the call feeling that I was knocked sideways.

I reduced into tears. Is that the same man who craved to hear my voice? Is that the same guy who preferred not to witness a tear in my eyes? Is that the same soul who cherished every deed of mine? I wonder if there cast a magic spell! He can't even presume how deep the sword that he poked into has pierced my body. He will never understand the damage he had done. I was into a sad state of affairs and faced the music for my mistake.

I deleted all his contact numbers. Blocked him on all the social media, I cleared his chat. I had his pictures around 20, I was about to destroy them, but soft-corner somewhere around me ceased doing so! I strictly restricted myself not to see, text, talk nor bother about any of his actions. I determined to empty his memories and formatted my brain.

It has been two months since I have remembered his thought. I however felt the heaviness in one of the rims of my heart for not conceding him. But his acts didn't make me regret. I was okay with my life. I moved on. I neither loved him nor liked, all I had is an addiction, which is more dangerous than any other.

It was one evening, Sathwika and I went to our spot to revive from the boring lecture in the intermission. This time, I sat and she was talking to me. Our talk initiated commenting on a junior who was passing by our way, we don't seriously comment on the face but uttered to ourselves, which gave more satisfaction. A junior girl, who was tall, and stout came to me and stood in front, I was like a tiny ant ahead an elephant. She was asking me the direction of the canteen and I was looking into her eyes and dictating the tracks as if I was on the ground floor and she was on the third floor. Sathwika burst out into laughter. I led her the way and was back to Sathwika.

She continued to giggle recapitulating the way I seemed near her. And I was like, sitting to a corner placing my hand over my face in helplessness. Then came a group of boys from the Mechanical department. I just nonchalantly inclined my head towards that way and it was Ram, after so long time, I had an eye to eye contact. I was melted a bit but then recollected that night and buried myself back. I didn't aspire to face him, so we vacated that spot, making our absence in their return to that place.

I tried to bring out a long-lasting relation, in that process, I left myself and led present relations nullified! All I could do is console myself thinking that it was water under the bridge.

MY GALLONS OF GOLD

We have been scheduled for a sudden vacation due to the outbreak of Corona. I still wonder how the human era now is locked in a battle against something, which is five million times tinier than us. Whatever, I'm both excited and anxious, happy that we were given holidays and sad that we were not declared adequate information regarding the deadline for the vacation. I packed everything and choose to go by bus that is being provided by the college than my father coming from so long way in this pandemic.

It was March 18, as my birthday is on March 22, I invited Parnika to come directly to my place without heading her home town. She even accepted my invitation. We boarded the bus that night, it was 12:45 a.m we sprang. We reached Kakinada at 4:30 a.m, we boarded another bus to my village. My dad called me, to know my status and asked me to ring him back once I reached the bus stop to pick Parnika and me. By the time I got down, my dad and my brother's friend were ready with their bikes to take us home. As I saw my dad, my eyes were ignited. Parnika and I got on my dad's bike and our luggage was carried on another bike. They pulled out their bikes.

We reached home at 5:00 a.m, my mom and Surya were waiting near the entrance for our arrival. As soon as we got down the bike, my mom greeted Parnika and then started describing my traits continuously,

"My baby, you grew so lean. Are you eating or not? And your complexion diminished. Is it only you or all the students over there alike? My God ! you became skinny and your hair got completely unconditioned."

Then Surya took his turn, "Maa, please stop it, she is dumbu chunky and you are saying that she became slender! She was born dark, how can you expect her to be fair now? And hair, she neglects her hair to air and never tied it up nor applied oil ! Don't expect something better when she does such acts," he criticized.

Then came, my mom to rescue. "Stop it, idiot, she had undergone a drastic change."

I then thought, I am never gaunt to my brother and never round to my mom.

We went in, had a shower, then breakfast. I am never comfortable with that strenuous bus journey and we didn't have a proper sleep too due to the roller coaster ride. As we were done with breakfast, my mom advised us to take a nap. Both of us slept till 1:00 p.m, my mom came to wake us up to have lunch.

We were then having meal, chicken curry, fish fry on the menu as I love non-veg. It was a sudden outburst of the topic about me, Parnika was pleading my mom to tell about my childhood episodes. My mom then said she would say one of the incidents that took place in my grade 10. As I heard that, I took an opportunity to narrate my story. I gulped food into my mouth and unfolded...

That Monday morning, we four, my dad, mom, younger brother and, I was supposed to attend the puja, that is being held in the nearby temple, a part of Dasara. As my mom was too devotional, we were to go to the temple with empty stomachs, as if God would allow only if we have a void in our tummy! It was around 4:30 a.m, we started our journey towards the mandir. It isn't too distant, just a walkable reach, takes around five minutes on foot. We arrived at the temple, the priest said that it would take exactly ten minutes to commence the rituals. We four took our places next to one another, my brother followed by my dad, then comes my mom, and finally me. People started coming, gradually the hall got filled and the priest handed over the mike to begin the puja.

My mom was into the holy world, completely immersed in the priest's words. My father and I were watching each other and smiling. Then, he hushed me not to do so putting his forefinger onto his lips insisting me to zip my mouth. I then concentrated on the priest's sayings. We were almost in midway and all of a sudden, the priest asked us to stand and revolve around ourselves for three rounds, it is probably a portion of the puja. I rose up and started revolving. I was okay with the first round but felt heavy standing, the second round was like, I got everything blurred, couldn't consistently stand and I fell unconscious abruptly on to the iron mike stand with a sharp edge which is placed on the transparent tiled floor.

I passed my fingers onto my mom's hand and said that I couldn't stand, with a heavy tone. This is all I could remember before slipping. By the time I opened my eyes, I felt some water droplets on my face. Wiping them provided me a clear scene to witness a huge crowd in front. I could still point my parents and my brother in that mass. They weren't those delighted profiles that I see daily but were startled today. I tried to get up from the base that I'm lying on but the density of my body didn't support!

Somehow, my mom lifted me. She asked if I am okay and she checked. I said, I'm but a little pain in the left part of my skull. I felt better getting up, I squatted beside my mother. I wanted to rest my head, I couldn't handle my weight. I laid my head on the lap of the girl who was perching next to me. She mildly rubbed my scalp comforting me. She loosened my hair, gently observing the injured part.

I could hear her words, "Oh my god, it is an extremely severe cut on her head and was bleeding." The mike stand which had a sharp edge pierced my skin and the blood oozed out. My mom heard those words from that girl and she checked the cut. She was appalled as she saw my internal partition. It was some portion of my brain that she could witness. My mom burst out into tears.

My dad after watching this left the puja amid, held me into his arms and was gushing to the hospital. The doctor said, "No tablet nor an ointment would work, she has to take stitches." I was yelling out and sobbing in, listening to the doctor. I was such a pampered girl in the family who wouldn't stand to the hurt, not even minimal. Watching the oceans in my eyes, my dad brought me back home. Each of my family members was persuading me to take up stitches, but I couldn't at least consider their words. My papa was into the bedroom, my mom into the kitchen, and my brother into the balcony.

I thought, they lost their patience in asking me and hated as I said NO. I went to the bedroom, I was struck seeing my dad weeping. I didn't expect this to befall, even my mom and brother were! That notorious brother who teased me all day long was shedding tears for me! I didn't ever want to be the reason for their sorrow but today, I am! I went to the hospital, slept on the gatch bed holding my dad so tight. The injecting of anesthesia pained me. I slowly fell asleep. I went to the hospital screaming and returned home smiling.

This is the story of grief in my life that strengthened me! I finished my food and the story too. Parnika listening to that, was silent for a moment. I felt guilty for making her sad sharing my sorrow. Then mom took the charge and taunted me with few names of those boys who proposed to me. Parnika laughed out loud. I loved it. My close ones in the same place, that too in joy, wished to last it long.

I was born rich, not in terms of wealth but got a family that values more than gallons of gold. If I have to choose one among heaven and my family, I would gladly go with the second option. The best thing I always love about my family is that every single idea is taken into consideration. They wouldn't neglect if the thought is from my younger brother, though he is younger, his notions were also into actions making them as a priority. I never took a chance to hide something from my parents. My sleep would hate me if I conceal anything, it wouldn't let me take a nap. I feel very free sharing my things with them. Then, why did I disguised Ram? It is just because I was not sure of the conclusion about him. I said to my mom that he likes me and is a very good friend of mine.

It is March 21, we slept that night and my nap was interrupted by a phone call from one of my friends to wish me on my day. Before I answer the call,

Parnika hugged me tight and wished. Then asked me to attend the call and kissed me on my forehead. The day has come, March 22. My 20th birthday welcomed by many calls one after the other. I was worried that my teenage came to an end but amused that I'm into 20. I answered the calls till 1:00 a.m and replied to a few texts, I checked for his message but failed to witness!

I woke up in the morning and was wished by my family. I got ready in my new outfit, as I came from the room, the cake was set in the hall. My brother didn't celebrate his birthday on March 12 as he was away from home and was attempting his intermediate examinations. He said he would rejoice it on March 22. I was drowning in happiness.

The cake got both our names in it and was adorable. It was strawberry flavor pastry, pinkish all over with green-leaved cream carved so perfectly. Our names brought out a special look to it. This cake made me lick my lips. We partied so well with all the cheers at home. And this was the first birthday to celebrate at home after four years of my departure to the hostel. I have no bounds for my emotional state.

Parnika and I have a separate world, we were like too intimate and she laid her shoulder when I'm drowsy. She ate all the healthy food just to make me habituate to it. Roasted me on my face but then smashed people for being the reason for my tears.

How wouldn't I thank God for giving me another me!

She always made no bones about boasting our friendship. We always had a conversation,

"What if our husbands don't allow us to meet after marriage?" I asked.

"Let us forget!" she said.

"What? Our friendship!" I exclaimed.

"No, our husbands," she answered.

We always had a fruitful time enjoying each others' company.

I planned a lot to do on my birthday with my best friend but the government didn't approve. It was declared a curfew. I felt a bit moody but, that made me spend time with my loved ones.

If I have to mention about my family, I was coddled from my childhood and even helped to cuff my shirt sleeves by my dad, he still makes me learn. I am 20 nevertheless a child to him. Twenty or fifty, we are always a kid to our dad.

Lovable SHE restricted ME to put on traditional fitments.

Then, HE supported me to go with my comfort.

He held my little finger,

little isn't little at all in fact,

shielded me with incredible love.

Deep in my comfortable sleep,

his tough and effortful fingers cleared

My messy hair all over my face.

With a lot of completeness,

kissed me on my forehead.

Hope that might have filled his tummy!!

His joy in my mischievous acts,

his tears in my pain,

his pride in my success,

his starvation when I'm hungry,

his smile when I'm happy.

That dearest hero of mine is my DAD!

If I have to put my love towards my dad into words, this would be an atom that I can express in this life where I still have molecules and elements to reveal!

The only thing that ruminated me was his missing greetings. I thought he would wish me, waited until the very last moment. But he didn't! Why should I fret for a stranger who didn't at least greet me on my special occasion, when I have the strength of my ever-loving ones near me? I expected both healthy and poor memories of his' to erase out of my brain like before. He is no more special!

MY EXCITEMENT IS SHORTLIVED!

Soon after my birthday, the pandemic in our area grew critical, we were not permitted out. Parnika got locked at my place and before the situation gets worse, she wanted to be back in her hometown. Somehow uncle arrived and drove her the very next day. I enjoyed her company at my home as I did it at college. I felt like, there is something unfilled in and around because of her absence. I got completely deviated from him with her presence. Once she left, I had the same monotonous cycle at home, waking late, skipping breakfast and jumping into lunch, holding a nap at noon, watching T.V, then dinner, ultimately sleeping early and this loop remained with no spice.

Then my neighbor named Usha and another tenant in the upstairs named Valli aunty asked me to join for the shuttle in the evening. I went too bashful on the first day. Slowly my timidness faded and was extremely close sharing all sorts of issues. It was we three who commenced playing out, gradually, the number got developed to another three, later two more kids added. We didn't bind to a single sport, even began playing throw ball, cricket, seven stones, skipping, hide and seek. These games made us recollect our childhood remembrances.

We were just satisfying with games that we were playing, but we wanted to play accurately and dug trenches to place poles for knotting the net for the shuttle and throwball as well. We strived a lot and somehow successfully laid the two poles that we wished to. Progressively, we marked the borders and made it our ground. It was green pasture all over, with fresh air streaming in the right direction, with the noise that kids made while playing brought out an exceptional glow to it. It was we who produced new rules when we were about to lose the game and those hyperactive kids never coped up with our precepts.

My attention swiftly stirred my appearances and physic, I am certain that I would turn bubbly in this lockdown. I became self-obsessed, concentrated much on looks. Usha and I intended to go on for a walk in the evening to balance our weight. We didn't miss a single day and were very punctual.

Gradually, our schedule was amended where we thought of rising early and were prepared for a morning walk, this was supplemented by exercise and yoga too. What can something do when we are dwelling at the determination? Usha woke me up early in the morning by a phone call. We even exchanged our contacts. We seriously wanted to lose weight. Valli aunty joined us after a couple of days. I, being not so plumpy went to walk just to maintain as it is because I always had a concern of turning chubby.

That evening, I was standing out and witnessing the sky,

The black clouds making the world dark, but I'm pacific!

The ghastly wind sweeping everything, but I'm pacific!

The terrible thunders roaring out, but I'm pacific!

The horrible lightning blazing it's light all over, but I'm pacific!

A pluviophile would appreciate the worth in waiting!

I remained for the rain to brush my clear skin that craved for the proximity of raindrops and the petrichor. That eventide, we didn't go to the ground as it got totally drenched with rain.

Rain…rain.. go away, come again another day…I could hear kids singing those rhymes. It was a booming sound, a thunder that brought a quietude in the atmosphere. All those songs were shut down. We turned out to have a short circuit in our locality and were into dark and deadly silence.

"LOOSE…!"

This reverberated in the peace that the thunder brought. It was Surya who was watching that scene on his mobile. Hearing that, my mind drove me into his intrusive thoughts. Usually, the best memories come out in the worst situations. I felt it right at the moment. I immediately vacated the place.

It was April 3, that evening, I was comforting myself on the sofa. My mobile beeped. I indolently stretched my hand to pull my mobile from the cupboard that was on the right side of the sofa. I grabbed my mobile, it was a notification from phone pey. I dragged the widget down. A notification from him that too on phone pey! This initially alerted me, I immediately stood in an attention mode. I brushed my eyes to check if I was interpreting perfectly. And it is from him, what I noticed is a hundred percent true. The first text from him after a long-span of three months melted me completely.

Once I got confirmation, I was bouncing with joy inside, almost dancing like a monkey. I was flooded with amusement. Without addressing a reply, I held the phone in both my hands and was contemplating. I captured a screenshot of it without opening the chat and sent it to Parnika. I expressed all my delight and enthusiasm to her. I hit somersaults internally and externally too. She was first struck then laughed for him to text on phone pey.

"Didn't he get any other social media to text. I'm pitying my dearest brother," she said and asked me to reply.

As I got a text from him, I forgot everything and wished to welcome.

I went into the chat screen,

"Midhunaaa," he first texted with two confused emojis followed.

"!!!!" was my reply.

"Hope you know me, do you?" he asked.

"I can see your profile and name over here," I said.

"Okay," he texted.

"By the way, do you know me, or did you text by chance?" I asked lifting my brows.

"I don't text people by mistake," he answered.

"Fine, what brought you here?" I questioned.

His answer slowly set a fire within me.

"I got a text from an unknown number threatening me for following her sister. As I received that, I texted her back inquiring if her sister is you, providing your name! I inspected for her on Facebook, I found that she is from the same school that you studied. So, I confirmed and

texted so! I checked for her profile on the true caller, to my surprise she is the elder sister of a lady from our college, and that girl is our parallel and your department. Later, I realized that I was overlooked. I'm sorry," he explained the whole thing that happened.

It was like pouring oil on flames. I was burning inside but pretended that I don't care at all.

"That isn't me. It's okay," I ended the conversation.

Who the hell is that lady to text him so? Is she crushing on him! I don't understand why girls are crazy about my man?

After monitoring all the information that he gave, I concluded that it was Pragna who is from the same place as I do and stays in the adjacent wing of mine. She isn't that pretty, though she isn't, I don't wish other girls to heed him. Call me jealous but I don't care! I heard it from some random girls that she had an immense crush and used to follow Ram in the college fest too. Recapitulating these, a monster arose in me, I thought of warning her but doing so will show us to people. They would bake rumors and encourage gossips that will set us down. So, I stopped!

This incident shifted my concentration back to him. I reread our previous chat and smiled in between. Step by step, this nullified my anger. I realized, it isn't that easy to switch our interests. I didn't find a plan to deflect. I sat in one of the corners of my house, with my mobile in my hand, staring into space and, traveled to the day when our journey commenced. I felt our story as the most trivial one and had a lot of twists to be turned.

I had a dream of being an emulous young writer from a very early age. But then, didn't find the exact zone that fits me. And today, I was struck with an idea of putting our journey as a story.

Exactly after three days of this episode, that is April 6th, I started. Writing our story was like bringing the stars down and putting them on the PC screen. I found this as the classic solution for altering my attention from him. Every word, every sentence that I planted was taking me to those days and my dimples were deepening bringing a curve on my face. Till then, I centered on my attire but then transformed it into my writing. My efforts to script our story lead me astray from the workout.

A WRONG NUMBER TO A RIGHT PATH

"You don't always need a madly running truck on the road to kill a love story; many a time people themselves are more than capable of killing their love stories", I was involved reading Ravinder Singh's novel, Can Love Happen Twice. These holidays made me addict to Ravinder Singh and his books. I was oblivious to the time connecting to his writings. I made my WhatsApp about VERY BUSY as I am in a hectic schedule reading. I rested novels for a moment and switched myself to WhatsApp. That day, it was Rishitha, who texted me,

"Hey, what's your about?" she asked.

"I changed it very casually," I replied.

"Even Ram got the same one," she said.

It was a bit peculiar but,

I replied, "Hope it has accidentally coincided and I deleted his number so long ago and have no clue about him."

"It is not unintentionally done, I found both of your abouts rivaling thrice," she said.

"It's better you question him, he would have an answer," I added.

"I asked but he is not online."

"That's okay," I concluded.

After half an hour, I was back to chat with Rishitha.

"Hey, any response?" I inquired with eagerness.

"Yeah, but he said, he doesn't have your number and stated something logicless. He even mentioned that you guys are not talking to each other," she replied.

"Ahh," I was grinding my teeth.

"By the way, why are you distanced?" she asked.

"He would have an explanation for this too," I mentioned.

"He would never say," she stated boldly.

Anyways, I prized her saying so, because, it made myself and my actions secure at him.

So then, I proceeded with a sketch to experience the craziness that he had towards me. He previously knew that I didn't save his contact because of which he would not view my display picture. I used this shot and made my WhatsApp privacy robust with few alterations. And they are, I changed my privacy settings to nobody on my profile picture, which means, nobody would have access to see and recorded his contact as CC. I executed this because those contacts I record, will usually have ingress to see my profile and no other would. I formulated an illusion for him that, his contact number was not saved. Then, I made my profile picture null and began editing my WhatsApp about. I didn't mind myself creating this just to feel the passion he had. And the fun is yet to come, I waited.

I adjusted it VERY BUSY. He even made the same followed by a smiling emoji. Then I replaced it with NOT AVAILABLE after half an hour. And he too changed it after a few minutes. Don't know what concerned him, he started answering to my WhatsApp about since Rishitha had noticed. I then turned my about, BATTERY DIED. He replied this with REPLACE IT WITH NEW 1 on his about. I was fierce but all right. I loved changing, it seemed like an online war. Then I came up with the message that I wanted to convey to him. And it was, KEEP IT PRIVATE TILL U KNOW ITS PERMANENT. Then, comes his response on my screen, NOTHING IS PERMANENT. It was seriously like a counter-strike on each other. I was digging it.

My enjoyment was hindered by my brother, he called me out to have lunch. I had a very delicious lunch, fish as the main menu, perfectly grilled besides, fish soup with white rice. My tummy was contented with the food. I went for dessert, I always had fruit since it is summer. There was a very strict rule implemented by my mum to have fruits, I indeed had options to choose best among those I hate, oranges, muskmelon, watermelon, blueberries, bananas, guavas, apples, mangoes and grapes. I took an orange and went into the bedroom.

I charged my PC and began where I have stopped, halfway from the first chapter of this book. There were butterflies in my belly when I was memorizing those days. I still fancied them to continue. I was like falling for him. Someone said, "Your crush has a secret crush on you" and I made it valid for him. He became my CRUSH. I craved to speak to him. But found no way to approach. As I held at crush, I made my about as, I IGNORE IF SOMEONE SAYS, I USED TO HAVE A CRUSH ON U CUZ, I HATE EXPIRED CRUSHES. It was his reply after 10 minutes on his about. It produced a twinkle on my face and it was, USED TO followed by a wrong symbol. I flew into the air and came back to where I paused.

WHERE THERE IS A WILL, THERE IS A WAY, I heard someone whispering into my ears. I just finished the chapter "Dreams Decide Destiny?" and was in a pleasant mood with the output. What about my WILL!? I was churning my brain for a plan. I logged into WhatsApp. Then it was an idea to ponder. With no delay, I implemented it. Call it weakness or my effort to curb my ego.

Oye! , changed about.

Haa… , replied on his about.

From when have you been replying to me through about, I changed mine.

It was an emoji saying that I have no words.

I made my WhatsApp about to thinking emoji.

He made it to a sick one.

I again changed it to, From when have you been answering.

He maintained the same reply.

I asked him to check my status.

Then started the status war.

Anything to speak? I posted my status making it visible only to him.

No, he posted.

I am like a mad monkey that moment, I posted, then why is this for?

It is my wish and I change, he shortened.

Then choose another girl and her about to reply, I countered.

It's all done and do you have any problem with that, he questioned.

Yeah, I said.

Okay sorry, was his response.

I posted, it's okay.

And found no reply.

With a lot of anger, I deleted his contact number again. And this is the conclusion of my WILL. Is that satisfying? No, Not at all, I wanted him to be sugary, not as if he was now!

I was burning like a volcano but that didn't stay for a longer time. I wanted to send him the chapter that I finished, so that he would be sweet. I caught my phone, posted it to Parnika first, then she asked me to wait for the review and I waited.

I texted her again to check if she is done. But, she isn't.

I could not resist myself, I am deadly curious to know his reaction after reading it. As per my knowledge, I could remember *8978, only five digits from his contact number, and to know the rest, I opened phone pey and checked it then, saved it in a hurry. *897884934 and named it CC and initiated the chat.

"I thought of informing you from a long time, please have a look at the attachment that I provide you below," I texted - 3:15 sent!

I made it a document and sent it.

As I forwarded, I noticed the double gray ticks. I have nothing to say but very excited to learn his reply. I was holding my breath for the gray ticks to turn blue.

In between, I got a reply from Parnika stating that it was fabulous. With that reply of her's, I am on tenterhooks and I started predicting his answer.

What would he say? Would he forget everything that happened and reply with a heart symbol? Or Will he fire on me as I mentioned his name and ID? Or Will he stay dumb? I was lost in my thoughts and didn't notice when the ticks grew blue. I didn't covet him to reply immediately but wanted him to take time and read it thoroughly. I too started reading the doc, imagining he was reading the text the same moment. I finished, but couldn't find a reply on my screen. Parnika took fifteen minutes to complete but why is he taking too long time, I churned my brain. Maybe, he is feeling the inner essence and rendering the past, I made up my mind. It is 3:45 p.m, I thought, he wasn't interested to reply and got mad at me. The very next minute, at 3:46 p.m,

I sent him another text, "I sent you this just because I applied your name in it. And it's just a part of my writings, don't mind."

Hope you are done reading.

It was my last text and deleted the doc that I sent him!

I was disappointed with his doings. I reread the messages that I texted him and I am like, displeased with his acts.

What kind of creep he was! I have to get out of a man like him. Arrogant idiot! Anyways stupidity is all mine to text him first! I started blaming myself. I opened the chat and checked his number, then the phone pey chat, there I got note of his number once again.

My pupil enlarged, I was appalled and sat straight on the chair.

Yeah! stupidity is all mine !! I SAVED A WRONG CONTACT !!!

*897884924 was his number and I, with my exhilaration made a crap with the last three digits!

I didn't know what to do …! I checked in true caller for the wrong number that I saved, it is **Devarakonda Ventakaramana!**

I immediately saved Ram's number with no error this time from phone pey and texted him in the following way,

"Hey, I texted some guy thinking it was you. The problem is not with the text but I sent him the doc

where I mentioned your name, Instagram ID, everything I did," I exclaimed.

I sent him the screenshot of the text I made. And I even sent him the document.

Then came his reply, "Don't worry, nothing will happen!"

"Everything was on my plate now. How shall I proceed?" I asked anxiously.

He asked me what number I have saved. Looking at the creepy task I made, he replied with laughing emojis.

"Hey monkey, why are you laughing? I am nothing from today," I said.

"If you get any messages or calls from that number, tell me, I'll speak to them, okay?" he asked.

I said, "Okay but I'm tensed."

He then said, "Wait for a second, I'll message them."

I said, "No, if that troubles you, I'll be affected much."

He replied, "Okay," with unsatisfying emojis.

I asked him to change his Instagram ID so that the wrong number would not connect him.

In the beginning, he said NO, but then okay was his reply.

Then he asked, "Is there anything that you could speak?"

I said, "NO," and the conversation ended.

He asked, "Tell me if there is any message or call from that number."

I said, "Okay," and he concluded bye along with TWINKLE, his emoji.

I got a scintilla of a smile on my face and that made me reply, bye with my SWEETY! Anyways, this wrong text was like a shot in the arm for me to text him after so long lapse.

I looked back to those words he texted,

"Text me if you get any messages or calls from that number."

I can only message him when I notice some alerts from that unknown number. So what shall I do to receive messages from it? Can I text that stranger whom I have unknowingly messaged once? Shall I repeat the same blunder?! No, I shall think of another approach. I blazed a trail, it is a blend of creativity, love, and is a bit notorious too. I immediately implemented it.

I installed dual WhatsApp on my mobile with another number that I use extremely rare and it was my father who only contact me through it. He isn't responding to your number, will he answer if you use another WhatsApp? My inner voice questioned. I made it clear with further proceedings. I texted from the newly installed WhatsApp to my original account. But what if you get a message from this account, all you need is a text from the stranger. My internal speech raised. What if, I make my new account as stranger's account?! I answered a question to my internal monologue. My brain thought I was out of mind observing my acts but after I finished my task, it discovered there is a method in my madness. It ended distrusting and bowed down wishing me good luck and departed. The texts that I made from the new account to mine read,

*"Hey, the story you wrote is awesome. Shall I get the continuation? By the way, I am the child of the one who possesses the number *897884934," I texted as a stranger to my account.*

"I am sorry, I sent you by mistake. I was to post it to my friend. Please don't' mind," I replied to my text.

"Fine, it's okay. Please forward me the continuation," stranger texted.

I didn't reply and got the possibility to text him.

*"Ram, I acquired a text from another number. The one who possesses *897884934 is his/her father. So the child read our story and texted from their number. Just a second, I'll send you the screenshot of our chat and the number," I texted innocently.*

"What?! Is that a girl or a boy?" he asked me.

"I don't know, shall I ask?" I asked him chuckling inside.

"No! I'll take care of everything and you don't worry. I just received the screenshot," he said.

"Okay, but what if it is a girl?" I asked bringing the vertical furrows between the brows.

"Nothing, I'll get committed," he said.

"I'll kill you, idiot," I texted.

"Just say it is my mistake and clear everything, nothing more," I ordered.

"Fine, I'll contact in the evening," he said.

"Okay, bye," I concluded.

I remained for my new account to beep. It was such a notorious task I have ever done. I suddenly rose, a doubt that hit my brain, Am I doing something wrong? Everything is fair in love and war, I got a reply from the space. I smiled but then corrected love to like. I am not loving him, not even he! We just like each other, but the fact here is he doesn't know I too liked him.

The delay had hit its end, it was a text on my new account.

*"Hello bro, the one whom you have texted for the continuation of the story is my friend. She texted you by mistake. It is *897884924, she is supposed to message, but in confusion, she pinged *897884934. Unknowingly altered the last three digits," he texted.*

"By the way, a small correction, I'm not bro," the stranger replied.

"Okay, I don't know. Anyways please don't trouble her. Don't even text her," he said.

"What hurt did I cause? I just requested for the second part as I felt impressive," told the stranger.

"There is no continuation. She penned it for pleasure," he stated.

"Anyways, who is that guy in the story. I wanted to see his picture. Can I get it?" the stranger asked.

"Just leave it," he denied so friendly.

"I didn't ask anything illegal. Just a picture!" the stranger said.

"The one in the story is me," he clarified.

"Is it!? So you are Ram?" stranger questioned.

"Yeah, and your good name?" he questioned back.

I was thinking for a name, suddenly hit with Sweccha and named my new account.

"I am Sweccha," she replied.

"So, picture?" she asked.

"Some other time," he said.

"Where do you live?" she asked.

"Vizag and you?" he answered.

"Guntur," she replied.

"Are you studying or passed out?" she interrogated.

"I am pursuing BTech second year."

"And what about you?" he added.

"I am doing my CA in masterminds."

"What is her name, the one who drafted the story?" she texted back.

"Midhuna," he replied. Seeing my name typed from him, made me bloom.

"Nice name. Is she loving you?" she asked.

In a flood of many laughing emojis, came the answer,

"Love?! Don't even try to get this topic near her. She would explode like an atom bomb," he said.

I laughed out listening to him.

"Do you love her?" she asked. I'm sincerely waiting for his reply.

"I don't know what I am up to, but I like her so much. She is ineffable," he said.

This instant, I wouldn't know pain though he poke me with serrated spikes. And I started coloring up.

"Is that? Did you say her?" Sweccha asked.

"Yeah, long back."

"What did she reply?" she questioned.

"She never provided clarity. She would smile for every expression of my love towards her," he said.

My stomach ached to laugh.

"What is your story? I love listening to love stories. Can I know yours?" she pleaded.

"You won't easily understand. It had a lot of twists and turns. Such a long one," he said smiling.

"I'm all ears. I am excited," she expressed her excitement.

"Shall I narrate you the next morn, its high time," he texted.

"Sure, good night," she said.

"Good night," he ended.

"Hey, don't text her," he reminded.

"Okay," she said smiling.

I was outlining what to ask the next morning. It was his message to my account in the dawn.

"Midhuna, I texted her and you will not face any problem further," he said.

"Is she a girl!? You messaged her! What did you say?" I acted frowning knowing everything.

"Yeah, she is a lady," he replied.

"Don't text her anymore, I'll take care of it. You just delete her contact," I told him.

"Okay, do you have anything else to say?" he asked.

Albeit I have, I'll ask you through that account, I said myself and smiled.

"No, nothing," I ended.

THAT MORNING

"Good morning, Ram," Sweccha wished, initiating the text.

"I just texted her and she would surely ping you back," he said.

"Message me! But why?"

"Just to warn you not to text me," he elated.

"I think she likes you, Ram. She is quite possessive."

"I don't hope so."

"Can I chat with her to know the answer?" she asked.

"First try to face her, she would yell at you for sure," he said.

Meanwhile, I texted Sweccha for messaging him.

I said, "I don't like, if some girl speaks to my close friend. I hate you doing so. Please stop texting him."

I conveyed my inner feeling just to make him know.

Then it is Sweccha who was saying these words to Ram,

"Your girl just texted me, she is aggressive. She cautioned me not to text you," she said to him.

"Is that? I am sorry for her disgraceful behavior," he texted.

It is humourous to listen to that sorry. I was relishing it. I still wanted to acknowledge his feelings towards me. Not everyone will get a chance to comprehend the love that one had on us that too, directly from him.

"That's okay," Sweccha replied.

"So, tell me about Midhuna," she added.

I wanted to know what he feels for me and so is the question.

"What do you aspire to know about her? She is an untold story," he said blushing.

"Is she pretty?" she asked.

"Pretty!? she is vivacious, almost eighteen members proposed her!"

"My goodness, I want to see her. Do you have a picture?"

"I'll send you some other time," he answered.

"What about her character?" she doubted.

"She is a bit insane," he stated.

"Insane! Isn't she genuine?" she posed.

"She is a benevolent and such a nice person I have seen to date. She wouldn't elevate her head when she steps out in public," he cleared.

"Then, what is this insane?" she pretended chaos.

"She would never give clarity for any of my questions and just locks me with her smile. Does everything like a kid and she is never old to play with those dolls. She gave them names too," he announced.

I turned pink, my lips almost reached my ears.

DIVING DEEP...

"When did your story start?" Sweccha initiated the conversation.

"I saw her in my PUC but approached in my first year of BTech," he answered.

"What is the sweetest name you gave her?" she raised.

"I call her Crush, and she calls me Candy," he said.

"Candy Crush makes the best combo ever," she gave her opinion. I didn't get a possibility to tell him.

"Did you ever turn mad over her?" she questioned.

"Yeah, once. She irritates so well and she is a specialist in executing it," he answered raising his shoulders.

"I desired to ask her the same questions that I requested you. Can I?" she said her opinion.

I wanted to express myself, so it would be better if she asks me and I tell her. The bitter thing here is, it is me who have to text both question and answer. I started texting and switched immediately to my account, write, and came back. Honestly, it was such a challenging race I have ever been into.

"I'll not text your friend but can I text you?" Sweccha asked me.

"Yeah," I answered.

"So, what is your name?" she posed.

"Midhuna and your name please?" I said.

"Sweccha," she answered.

"Is Ram your classmate?" she asked.

"No, he is from another department. He is from the Mechanical branch and I am a Computer Science student," I told.

"Ram…! loves you?" she jumped directly into the topic.

"No! He is just crushing," I shortened.

"How did he reveal you?" she asked.

"He always said. Every time possible. He used to like me a lot, such an ingenuous guy he was," I said.

"Used to?! What does that imply?" she questioned.

"He used to like me, but now it is all faded. We fought and so we are," I explained.

"So, how can you conclude that he doesn't fancy you anymore?" she questioned.

"Sweccha…, we speak to those we like and ignore those we don't," I said.

Sweccha captured a screenshot and sent him. Looking at this, he was into aghast.

"Sweccha, witness her stupidity. I'm drowning here and there, she is declaring that I have no passion!? This is the reason why I call her Loose," he expressed his situation.

"How can she learn if you don't convey? Go talk to her," she advised.

"Yeah, I'll address within a week or two. If not she will nevermore understand my emotions," he told.

Hurray!! This is what I needed, ultimately, I made it. But I wanted this to happen quickly. I cannot wait for a week. I texted Sweccha that I am going to uninstall WhatsApp and didn't communicate her the reason. Now comes out love, flooding.

Am I pulling the wool over his eyes? I was again raised with a question.

Everything is fair in love and war, someone whispered. I corrected it changing love to like and smiled.

They both had a conversation and he decided to text me in the evening. It seems like a three man play but it is literally two!

"Any plan you had, to proceed?" she questioned.

"I will play it by ears," he said.

"Will she respond to you?" Sweccha asked.

"I'll blow her anger. I know how to placate her," he said winking.

"All the best," she wished.

I was anticipating for his text. I was besides checking my mobile. I couldn't find any of his notifications. It was almost two hours yore. But then I recognized that I didn't turn my data on. Hitting myself, I switched on.

"Crush!!" followed by grief emojis was his text.

Whatever the cause may be, but noticing his message on my screen brought out celebrations within me. I fired almost every firework. It is all Sweccha's perseverance that brought out a reunion.

I replied to him with a shocking emoji. Gradually, with his skill of melting me, he softened and we had a continuous chat for approximately three hours. I said everything that I wished to speak all these days. I first told him off for all his mistakes and then he said no word opposing me. Finally, I conveyed my confession, this brought down the burden that I'm carrying all way along. I am completely satisfied.

We were just like before, into our bond. Candy and Crush were back.

We had a halt-less conversation all day.

With the chat that Sweccha had with him, he finally declared that he loves me but all that bothered him is, I being hatred towards love. He didn't give an attempt to tell me. The moment he announced his love, I was touching the sky to bring stars down to compete with my glow. Of course, they wouldn't beat me right at the moment. I yearned to give him clarity concerning this and wanted to know his response.

Sweccha texted me, I, being a pragmatic person, gave a clarity saying a lengthy view.

"I will only like him if he convinces my dad. Loving a person for timepass is all scrap and I hate such relations too. Love's ultimate aim is to marry or else, it is of no use. If he loves me even after my BTech, he would get an opportunity to talk to my dad. I always had a soft corner towards him. I would accept his proposal. He is a genuine guy, had no immoral manners and I believe he would love me more. Finally, I enjoy his company moreover, he is handsome too. Will someone try to sacrifice him for any other girl? But this works only if my dad accepts him. I seriously pray God that Ram would not express his love now, only if he had. It would be better if he proceeds after our graduation."

It is not the time to wool-gather about the future but just handle the present. My heart urged.

I was ecstatic letting him know my feelings without my involvement. The Crush I had on him started developing.

When he is near me, I act unusual,

I watch him making others involved in their works so that, they would not mark me staring at him.

I rush out for his arrival as if I had work to do outdoor.

I communicate loud, people assume I am arrogant but it is to make him admit my voice.

I choose distance rather displacement because it makes me gape at him for a bit longer time.

But when he is incomparably away, after all, I just hold no words and stay dumb!

I penned this down on a friend's request, it even suits me at the moment.

He always expressed his love near Sweccha, I could relate his trails to convey to me but I always replied to him smiling. I didn't expect that my smile would put things to an end like it drops the topic with no conclusion. He evermore adored my name as I am possessing it.

I always put our photos together and state that we are made for each other only to those who wouldn't respond like the sky, breeze, shrubs. We are carved so well by God.

Having him in my life is like,

A mustard yellow t-shirt with a blue denim

A cookie with cream

A white plane with black checks

A movie with popcorn

A cup of custard with gulab jamun

Like we made the best combo ever!

He is so confident that he would convince my dad and papa would accept if Ram attains a good job. I am certain with his words.

Am I doing something wrong, pulling a fast one on him? The question raised again. But this time, nothing whispered.

EVERYTHING IS FAIR IN LOVE AND WAR but not in LIKE! I realized. But it's been high time that I have apprehended.

Anyways, I got to know everything that I needed and more than enough. I got a couple of his pictures too. It was my diligence that led to a peaceful ending of Sweccha's character.

"Ram, it is my brother's mobile that I am working on. And he is now leaving. I have no chance to learn about your story but for sure you would succeed. All the best. Take care of your little doll," Swechha texted and ended her chapter.

DECISIONS DECIDE DESTINY?

It was May 5. I was enjoying sweet sugary candies recalling my Candy. After I, knowing that he loves me, I couldn't have authority over my emotions. My heartbeat was continuously rising and falling. I could now recollect those texts he made trying to tell me his love.

Hey crush, you know what, I like you so much.

No matter what, I wish not to see you in moist eyes.

I promise you that, I will never get mad over you. You are my LOOSE.

You are not my crush anymore, you are beyond crush and beneath love.

I love her, Sweccha, but I don't know how she takes it.

I like her smile, it halts me all my way. Such a cute one she had!

I know, we always made the best pair.

I smiled and opened his photos that I saved. I was perpetually observing him, if my mobile had life, it would knock me hard for doing so. I collaged our pictures and scrutinizing them in every angle, if we made the best pair. I have no consistency. I was walking with no proper maintenance. What is this anxiety for? I don't still understand how he concealed his love for three years, so I am not! I could now realize it was hard to curb that urge. I rendered his silly acts.

At times, he walked after me without my notice,

but as I lean back,

he would behave as if he doesn't know me.

He gawks at me from a distance, as I get closer,

he would run as if a cheetah chasing him.

Some call it is stupidity, yet

very few understand it is fear of losing.

My heart was pushing me to proceed and brain was pulling me off. Should I listen to my heart or brain? Both pointed in opposite directions. Can I propose him first? How can a girl, that too, a girl like me proceed with a proposal, straight away? But I ached to convey him somehow. There is nothing wrong if you go ahead and no rule stated, it is only boy who should initiate a love proposal. It can even be a girl and wise girl like you can have the best starter. My monologue concluded and heart won the battle.

I led to a saturated point. Yes, ultimately I am supposed to assert my feelings towards him. I just wanted to call him. My heart was almost into pants. How would I? It is my skin that I could feel when I put my fingers in. Fine, what if I text him? Yeah, this is better. But what do I write?

Candy, I'm going nuts because of you. I love you!

I cleared the text in search of better words and thoughts.

You are the ingredient, my life needs daily, and your happiness gives my life fulfillment. I love you, Ram!

I again deleted thinking something better. The fickle-minded me, changed my views several times.

At a point of time, I was laughing at me for my deeds. What am I doing?

Dearest Ram!

I never imagined a day like this would come in my life. I feel the world spinning much faster than usual. You are such an amazing guy where I don't have any reason not to fall in love with you. The things you do, the way you call my name, convince me beyond doubts and you are the man of my dreams. I want to be with you, Ram, on this journey of life because I think I can't find a better partner than you. Life is precious, but you are more precious to me, and I love

you. You've gone the extra mile to make me yours. And now, you made it.

I love you, Candy!

Finally, I wrote. But what if I send it? I am on pins and needles, frazzled to send. I plucked up courage and sent. I went offline immediately. To sum up, what goes around comes around. It's love all over.

It was a heavy downpour that evening. My parents attended a housewarming ceremony as I always hated attending functions, I was struck home and had to take care of the household things by their arrival. I swept the rooms, then filled water bottles playing all my favorite songs in the background.

By this time, he would have read. He invariably wished to heed that from me. He will surely hit somersaults in exhilaration. I loved to hear him right at the moment and wished to share his joy. What will he reply to me? Will he break out in cold sweat? Or Will he reply with his acceptance. How will he reply? Will he expect this from me? I should put an end to questions and get into actions to pull out the answers. I switched on the mobile data with a lot of zeal. It didn't turn blue nor double gray ticks! What is he doing things offline when he had life concerns online? Even after two hours, there is no change. I waited with bated breath for him to read and reply.

I was frequently checking if there was a change with the ticks. Exactly 5 minutes later, I found gray ticks turning blue one after the other. I immediately came out of the chat and waiting for the beep. I set a countdown 10 9 8 7 6 5 4 3 2 and 1. It is 1 that I counted, I was dancing as if mad, my songs complimented too. I calmed down and opened the chat screen. I couldn't still find his reply. I thought there might be something wrong with the signal as it was heavily raining. I waited for a bit more time. I couldn't find anything progressive even after 30 minutes. To quick-fix the concern right now, I disassembled my mobile and arranged it perfectly so that if there exists an issue with the interior dissection, it gets cleared. I switched on and opened the chat screen. By the time I fixed, my parents arrived and they were completely drenched. I offered them a towel to wipe off the water, they changed their attire and my mom was about to prepare some snacks. And dad went to his room to work.

Maybe he was struck seeing my texts, let him take time to reply. Then, I went to have a shower expecting a reply by the time I come. I skipped dinner and rushed to turn on data. The optimistic me even failed this time witnessing no reply! What is this idiot doing? Fine, let him decide in one or two days.

I was like jumping out if I get any notification hoping that it was from him. I extended my patience for two more days frequently keeping an eye but found no reply in any sort of time. Is he taunting me as I didn't respond for his love those days, tit for tat!? All I could notice after a day of my proposal was, no display picture of his and no about written. I texted him concealing my anger for his recklessness towards my sensitive feelings. It was a single tick and found to be the same for three days. The forbearance got diluted in me. I called him leaving all the fears behind. I heard something that I didn't expect to hear.

The number you are dialing is currently switched off. Please try again later.

Why is he doing this to me! Did he block me on WhatsApp and switched his mobile off for sneaking himself near me? But what is this for? Did he pass time or truly loved? If he loved, what will this incautious behavior depict? I could now realize, he needed to get rid of me. I am not crying but the anger in me turned out resulting in the eruptions in my eyes. They are not just tears but is lava with intense heat. I entirely forfeited my solidity. All I could do is sob till the tears in my eyes dried.

I abruptly woke up from the doze wiping off my tears. Even my teardrops would not know the motive for their arrival. His reflections and phrases evoked me. They are not hiring me to sleep. I disassembled the cottage of LIKE that he erected. I didn't tolerate an atom survive in my soul. If it endures, I am clear that it would regenerate. I comprehended, if someone priorities you beyond the threshold, then margins are to be overcome for their utterance of love. His memories crumbled into the evocative ruins that I am experiencing.

The tears in my eyes rolled down but, I couldn't find a shore to stop. I only had my hand to wipe when I moaned. This flung me into a situation, where I had to choose seven from the dice. But when I hear his name, I try to bring a curve on my face thinking that it would set everything straight right at the moment. I texted him daily expecting a reply from him. Every deed I did for him is now taunting me. I am helpless.

My father once said to me, "If a man prefers you, nothing can resist him away." So a man who understands that, you want to hear from him, wants to be with him, and wants him to combat against your difficulties yet a distance is bringing a fairly apparent message, he's either ambivalent or he's no longer interested. It's a very ugly, passive way to regale someone you supposedly care for or once cared for and it's the coward's way to back out. One that minimizes their pain and involvement in a nameless relationship but that maximizes your pain and confusion.

He has plenty of opportunities to convey to me why he made this sudden and unprovoked termination, and he has chosen not to tell me.

My frustration level is undoubtedly at the top of the scale, unfortunately, there is nothing I can do about it. He may have some sound reason for cutting me off, one which has nothing to do with me or it may be a very silly or absurd one, which he was too embarrassed to say. Regrettably, I cannot force him to speak about it, and I was certainly not going to entice him to tell.

Of course, he owes me an explanation. However, that is not a debt he is going to pay. He has already made that clear with his actions.

I should conclude that the relationship doesn't mean very much to him if he can end it so abruptly. I should also recognize that if he is the sort of person who cannot even face up to me and speak his mind, that he is not the kind of person with whom it is worth having a relationship. He lacks the character or the maturity to speak honestly with me about whatever is troubling him, and that indicates me, I am well rid of him.

A big blow to my pride and ego, to be sure. But his abruptness and unwillingness to communicate suggests that I too should bring my interest to an immediate end in him. Making it a clean break, and go on with my life.

The demon in me, woke up and I deleted all my messages that I sent him and blocked his contact.

I once thought it is dreams that decides destiny but realized,

DECISIONS DECIDE DESTINY!

It was May 5. I was walking on the footpath stretching to the departmental store. RAM…! I felt like Midhuna calling me. It was sweet that overflows when she spells my name. It's damn difficult for me to turn out once I get into her thoughts. I opened the privacy locker and watching her photos. That winking picture, I always wish to be the one facing her at that moment. The way she poses putting her tongue out drives me crazy. There were 37 pictures that I saved and it takes around 30 minutes for me to switch from one picture to the other. I just lifted my head facing the sky to thank God for sculpturing such an innocent creature. I was mulling over her, then my mind flew to a day when I saw her.

She, with pretty brown eyes,

having a fair complexion.

With her silky black hair held loose

waving as the breeze direction.

She wore a white top with the same colored bottom

and is beautified with a peach dupatta

hung to her left shoulder.

Besides, with a winsome smile on her glossy, baby pink lips

which brought out an extra spark to her.

What am I about to?

All I could do is to remind myself to breathe!

I did not notice two motorcycle-borne miscreants following me and within seconds, a curly hair, dark-complexioned guy yanked my mobile and they sped away. Everything happened in an eye blink. I had nothing to do with the unfortunate that had happened with me. I chased him to an extent but I couldn't compete with the raise of the accelerator. I went home with a loss of my life. It is not because of the cost that my mobile possesses but her photos that matters to me much. My father filed a complaint against the snatcher and came home.

What if I install Instagram in my dad's mobile and contact her? That's a good idea. But then I remembered that she stopped using it. Even when she is right in front of me, I still miss her. Till to date, I watched her pictures which compensated her absence but what can I do now? I was staring the space thinking I would get an idea reaching her.

LOOSE...!

I heard this. I stood up and picked up to run into the hall. It was that movie where I could relate her. I always felt she lived in that scene. I wonder if this is the idea God gave me. I decided to watch this movie as many times as possible until I find my mobile. Every time I watched, I felt like all I need in life is my cute lady, and nothing is coming in between our love.

It was after three weeks, I got my mobile into my arms. And my heart was now out of fluctuation, I immediately took my mobile which was switched off. Maybe it is that man who turned it off to escape from the cops. I found everything new, that idiot might have reset my mobile, I lost her pictures that I saved. This worried me much than anything else. I installed WhatsApp. I found no display picture on her profile and no about too. Maybe she is fed of changing them and not everyone likes to post a picture on their profile.

I don't know what but the distance between us made my love grow and I reached my saturation point. This is the right time to choose her, don't know how she responds but I am unable to stay common. Didn't I ever feel like that? Of course, I felt, but it is a distance that brought the change. If I knew earlier that gap will alter, I would have distanced a long ago. I sincerely love to share my life with her, but the only fly in the ointment was her reaction, the way she takes it matters.

Yes, Ultimately I am supposed to assert my feelings towards her. I just wanted to call her. My heart was almost into pants. How would I? It is my skin that I could feel when I put my fingers in. Fine, what if I text her? Yeah, this is better. But what do I write?

I love you like the fish loves water.

I found some other thing better and removed midway.

You're my blue crayon, that never has enough of, the one I used to color my sky.

Is it dramatic?! fine I'll go with my feelings directly.

Dearest Midhuna,

I being an introvert, cannot express myself but somehow developed the courage to tell you this.

A Selenophile would not love the moon

if he had witnessed you.

A Hodophile would not have traveled

just the way I explored your heart.

A Nyctophilia would hate night

to see your arrival in the dawn.

What else would I say if my words drain?

I LOVE YOU MY DEAR CRUSH…!

I texted her, and was out of the chat. My feelings might have travelled bypassing all the cell towers, and satellites. I found a single tick on her chat, maybe she was offline. I still wonder how my stone heart turned soft seeing her.

I didn't believe in miracles till the day I saw her.

Her smile, that dainty one, kills me all my way.

At times, I felt like talking to her,

if that isn't possible, I made my friends listen to all my stories from the very beginning.

I know, my peers wouldn't feel like the way I do.

My face glows like a moon when

I had a little conversation with her.

My dream of meeting her at times,

is seriously setting me alive.

She is cashew in the cream.

Her simplicity, her uniqueness is all the evidence

for me to fall for her!

If I get a chance of conveying my things to her, I would have commenced from the day, I first texted her. I was trembling with fear to request her on Instagram. But then, I found Gowtham irritating her. If that idiot deserves to text her, why wouldn't I? Then rose my journey.

The day she gave me her contact number, I was genuinely thankful to all those who texted her on WhatsApp that instant. And it was God who conspired to union us.

That moment when she was narrating her ideal husband qualities, I related each quality to me. I felt as if she was stating about me.

I was boiling like water beyond its boiling point when she described her crush, Harshith.

The day she attended when I followed her, I wouldn't get such a moment though I spent dollars. Her looks overrode my senses.

Then, my birthday call, I wanted it to last but what if I make crap out of control? So I declined. I reminded that voice, she spoke just like a kid. Soon after she disconnected, I wished her to call me again. Within no time, I found my phone ringing, **CRUSH** calling… it was displayed on the screen. I was pinching myself if I was witnessing something true.

It was ridiculous pain that I have undergone to say NO to her words when she requested me to speak but it's all I could test myself, how far can I move back without loving her. My heart oozed with grief that day.

Finally, I found it is just three months that I stayed with no contact yet my soul was running behind her.

I wanted her so desperately, that made me proceed with a text which brought CANDY CRUSH back!

I always wonder how my yelling lady turns into an emotional one! Sensitive ones can understand this much better. The little things were important to her. Like this unique idea of ending a conversation with SWEETY and TWINKLE.

I waited for 3 three years yet waiting for her reply isn't a big deal and is so precious too. I will wait like a lantern in the clear sky for your call, my dear girl. The decision that I took now might change my destiny. Hoping that it would take me to the bed of roses into her world.

DECISIONS DECIDE DESTINY!

Best Is Yet To Come…!

www.ingramcontent.com/pod-product-compliance
Ingram Content Group UK Ltd.
Pitfield, Milton Keynes, MK11 3LW, UK
UKHW041345190726
13845UKWH00026B/429

9 789388 762243